MONSTROUS

Written by
CHARLOTTE BOND

To my constant friend,
Mark,

I hope you enjoy.

Charlotte Bond

Hersham Horror Books

Charlotte Bond

HERSHAM HORROR BOOKS
Logo by Daniel S Boucher

Cover Design by Neil Williams 2017
Copyright 2017 © Hersham Horror Books
Story copyright Charlotte Bond 2017
ISBN: 978-1545201343

The Primal Range
First Edition.
First published in 2017

Also from
Hersham Horror Books:

The Primal Range

Becoming David by Phil Sloman
Paupers' Graves by James Everington
Laudanum Nights by Stephen Bacon
The Factory by Mark West

Charlotte Bond

Dedicated to

My mother who always
believed in me

My father who introduced
me to Tolkien, HG Wells
and "Alien"

MONSTROUS

CHAPTER ONE

Jenny woke up but didn't open her eyes; if she did, she knew she'd have to talk to her mother. The movement of the car was soothing and her iPhone was playing a mellow playlist. Much better to hang onto the pretence of sleep a little longer.

But her neck was at an angle, and her back ached from too long spent in the same position. Reluctantly, Jenny shifted in her seat and opened her eyes. She looked out of the window, confused. They weren't on the motorway any more, but a straight, empty road with open fields on one side and scattered woodland on the other. She took her headphones off and sat up.

"You're awake, then," Pamela said.

"We can't be in Scotland already, can we?" Jenny asked.

"No." Pamela avoided her daughter's gaze and Jenny's suspicions grew.

"Is this a back road to Gran's house?"

No answer.

A sign came speeding towards them which read Alnwick 15 miles, Berwick-upon-Tweed 40 miles.

Jenny sat bolt upright. "What the hell, Mum?"

"Now, I was going to leave it as a surprise when we got there," Pamela said in a conciliatory voice, "but we're going to live somewhere different for a bit."

"Different? Where? How long is 'a bit'? Mum, what have you done?" Hot anger and cold dread wrestled inside Jenny.

"Let's wait until we get there, okay?" With that said, Pamela refused to be drawn any further.

Jenny slumped back in her seat, her arms folded. She glared out of her window. The grassland disappeared and more trees crowded along the verges until they were driving through a forest. Eventually, Pamela slowed the car and indicated left. Jenny squinted at the hand-painted sign next to the turning.

Haven.
If you lived here you'd be home by now!

"Isn't that sweet?" Pamela said.

Jenny answered with silence.

The road was tarmaced, but had clearly seen better days. The car bounced through potholes. Dense forest pressed close around them until they reached two tall stone pillars either side of the road, with a pair of high wooden gates standing open.

"Looks like the entrance to 'Jurassic Park'," Jenny muttered.

"I think it looks delightful."

Jenny recognised the tone, the one that meant her mother had come across a new fad and was going to cling to it until either the new idea didn't work out, or the man involved left her.

And she's dragged me along for the ride. Fucking great.

As they drove down the main road, Jenny saw side roads leading off into the trees. The narrower roads led to circular clearings, each with three single storey wooden lodges around their circumference.

The car came to what looked like a grand turning circle. In the centre was a large empty fountain, its centrepiece three leaping stone dolphins. Covered in green moss and black lichen, the dolphins looked more like creatures of the forest than the sea.

Pamela drove around the fountain and pulled up in front of a long, squat stone building with a slate roof. A faded red sign bearing the word 'Reception' was stuck in the window of the door.

A fragile hope rose up in Jenny. "You've brought us on holiday?"

Pamela gave her an enigmatic smile. "Yes, I suppose. This place used to be a holiday park, but it's a bit different now. We're on a working holiday, so to speak."

A working holiday didn't sound good at all. Pamela got out of the car and called a greeting. Jenny looked through her window and saw a tall man walking towards them from the reception building. He wore a thick jumper with a shirt underneath and clean jeans that contrasted with his muddy boots. The top of his head was bald, but beneath the pate was a semicircle of closely shaved grey hair.

Bald? That's a new one for Mum, Jenny thought. But she wasn't surprised; this man radiated confidence and charm. It took Jenny a moment to notice the small woman hurrying behind him. Unlike the man, who walked with his head up and shoulders straight, the woman's eyes were fixed on the ground and she hugged a clipboard to her chest. Her thin, mousy hair fell over her face.

Secretary or wife? Either way, what a pair.

Jenny caught the impatient glare that Pamela was directing at her. With a sigh, she hauled herself out of the car.

"Mrs. Riley," said the man, extending his hand as he approached. He shook Pamela's hand by clasping both of his around hers. Jenny was repelled to notice that his thumb stroked the back of her mother's hand.

Oh god, please let me be wrong. Don't let him be her latest crush.

"Mr. Vernon," Pamela said warmly.

Pamela tucked a strand of curly blonde hair behind her ear. Then she did her signature move, dropping her eyes to the ground so that she could look back up from under her lashes.

Oh god. It is. It's him.

"Please call me Thomas," he said with a beaming smile. His eyes flicked to Jenny as she reluctantly approached. "And you must be Miss. Riley," he said, offering her his hand.

Jenny crossed her arms in front of her, giving him a steely stare. His smile didn't waver, but he dropped his hand, sliding it into his pocket.

"I'm Jenny. Jenny Pine."

"Oh. My mistake. Whatever name you choose, you're welcome here with your mother."

"Where exactly is here?"

"Don't you know?"

"I haven't told her yet," Pamela admitted.

Thomas beamed. "Ah! The big reveal. Well, I won't spoil it for you. But I will say this: my wife and I hope you'll decide to stay with us after your trial period. Don't we, Anna?" He stepped back, putting his arm around the woman who hovered behind him.

"Yes. Of course," Anna said. Her voice was low and calm, but there was hostility in her gaze as she looked at them both. She proffered the clipboard. "If you could sign a couple of documents please, I'll get everything sorted. You're in Ash Lodge."

CHAPTER TWO

Dan stood at the door of the generator house, wiping his hands on an old rag. He surveyed the new arrivals. The woman had blonde, curly hair and wore tight jeans with a baggy jumper. The girl wore bootleg jeans and a hoodie. Her hair was a darker blonde and without the curls. It framed her scowling face. She looked like a troublemaker, but she also looked a similar age to him. It might be nice to have someone else his own age around.

"Checking out the new blood?" said a voice behind him.

Dan turned and grinned at Mick, the gatekeeper, who was walking towards him. Dan didn't know Mick's real age but he guessed it was close to about sixty; it was hard to tell when the man's wrinkles merged into his smile lines.

"Like you weren't," Dan shot back.

Mick cackled and scratched his head under his woollen hat. His clothes were always scruffy, but of a good quality, meant to last. Dan always thought the same was true about Mick himself. Mick's Alsatian, Apollo, sat down obediently next to his master.

Mick squinted at the distant figures. "She's got nice legs, but she's not my type. Women generally aren't." He gave Dan a calculating stare. "I didn't think they were your thing either. Or have I got that wrong?"

Dan swiftly looked away, a yawning black hole seeming to open in his mind. Despite the warm spring air, his skin prickled with goosebumps.

Damn it! I thought I'd hidden it so well.

But I guess if anyone was going to find out, it was going to be Mick.

Dan struggled for words to draw the conversation away from this potential moral mire. His gaze flicked to the little group as they headed towards the lodges. As casually as he could, he said, "Do you think that we should be taking in newcomers now? With everything going on?"

"Oh, so you think something's going on?" Mick's voice was taunting.

"Cut the shit, Mick. I'm not Thomas. I've got eyes and ears. There's something going on in Haven."

"You don't think old Millicent was imagining it then, seeing a hideous face at her window?"

Dan shrugged. "There were plenty of teenage vandals at my old school who went around with masks on so they wouldn't get caught. I bet standing outside an old woman's home, ready to scare the shit out of her with a mask is the sort of thing they'd find funny."

"So you believe Thomas then? That it's kids mucking around?"

"Yeah. It makes sense, I guess."

Mick stared into the distance. "I found a dead rabbit the other day. Normally there's only bones and fur left, possibly the odd limb. But this one was torn into pieces, each limb detached and carefully laid out. The head, front paws and back paws had been separated from the torso, then carefully arranged on the grass. Almost like someone had taken it apart before trying to see how it fit back together."

Dan shuddered. "Still could be boys."

"I used to be a forest warden. I've seen plenty of dead animals in my time, skinned some as well. I know the difference between a joint that's been sliced apart by a knife and one that's been pulled apart." He looked at Dan, his gaze intense. "That rabbit was ripped into pieces, still alive I'm guessing by the amount of blood there was. You have to be strong and determined to do that to a wild animal. That's not the work of errant kids. That's something different."

Dan dug out his rag and wiped his hands again, even though they were free of grease. He thought of the winter nights he'd walked through Haven alone. He remembered the feeling of being watched from the trees or hearing the rustle of something moving through the bushes. He'd put it down to paranoia. He thought of the strange scuff marks he'd found in the snow around the bins. He recalled the night he'd sanded down their front door while his mother was in bed, because he didn't want her to see the scratch marks that an animal had left there. The skin on the back of his neck had prickled as he'd worked, and he'd been constantly looking over his shoulder. Thomas's theory about kids couldn't hold up against evidence like that, but Dan was too afraid to consider what the alternatives might be.

Mick cleared his throat, breaking through Dan's thoughts and asked, "Maybe you'd like to join me on one of the night-time patrols? Get you out of that house. Night air is good for the lungs."

Dan sensed a hidden agenda behind the offer. He wasn't sure he wanted to get dragged into what was going on so he replied, "Yeah, maybe. I'll think about it."

Mick nodded and walked off, the dog trotting at his side.

Maybe it wouldn't be so bad to talk to Mick, Dan mused. *He seems fair and open-minded. Not like Anna or*

Samuel. Maybe talking to him would help sort out all this mess in my head about Haven and... other stuff.

Dan turned back to the generator, wishing he could find a way to dispel the dark cloud that hovered over him these days.

Jenny paced around the lodge while her mother parked the car in the commune car park. Everything Pamela had told her as they'd unpacked was going round in Jenny's head. She stared around the lodge, hoping to find something to distract her from her rising anger. The one storey lodge had a large open living area. The lounge, which boasted a battered TV, a couch and a wood stove, took up one third. An open area with a table and six chairs made up the dining room. The last section was the kitchen, separated from the rest of the room by an L-shaped counter, making it perfectly possible for whoever was cooking dinner to see and talk to anyone who was sitting on the sofa. At the furthest end from the lounge were three closed doors leading into other rooms, mostly likely bedrooms and bathrooms.

The whole place was spacious, clean and modest, even if it smelt stuffy. Jenny had to admit that she and her mother had stayed in worse places, but that thought only seemed to make her angrier, as if the welcoming nature of the lodge was another part of a conspiracy against her.

This is a fucking joke. It has to be. A self-sufficient commune? I can't believe she visited the damn place without me as well. She planned it all perfectly: she knew if she told me I'd talk her out of it, so she's just dragged me up here without a word. I'm going to fucking kill her.

The minute Pamela opened the door, Jenny said, "Just how long are you planning on keeping us here?"

Pamela closed the door and said calmly, "I'm glad that you're talking to me again, Jennifer, but I could do without your anger, thank you very much. And I don't know how long we're staying. I had to pay a deposit for the lodge—"

"A deposit? How much?"

Pamela stiffened. "Not much. It was covered by our savings with plenty left over for your college fees." Jenny groaned but Pamela continued. "It's just a trial thing, Jenny. Everyone joins for a few months, to see if they like it and if they fit in, and then a final decision is taken by the whole commune as to whether we can stay."

"And these people are, like, what? Hippies?"

"That's an unkind label."

"Label or not, are they?"

Pamela sighed. "If you think of them as hippies, you'll get completely the wrong idea. They are people with great morals and values, who care about the environment and want to go back to basics. This really is a fascinating place. They're still hooked up to the grid, but they have turbines and solar panels to provide most of their electricity. They collect wood for fires to keep the lodges warm. They have fields. One of them is a campsite in summer, others are rented out to farmers and some they use to grow their own food. What they don't eat they store or preserve or sell at farmer's markets. They have animals too: goats, horses, chickens, bees. You like animals, don't you?" Jenny glared at her but said nothing. "You'll get some real hands-on experience of caring for them while we're here. I bet that will look great on your CV. You always said you wanted to be a vet, didn't you?" Pamela's voice had an edge of desperation now.

"Oh, yeah, great. And just how do you expect me to be a vet when I'm stuck in the arse-end of nowhere? What school am I going to, Mum?"

Pamela nervously scuffed a bit of dirt with her shoe before giving Jenny a bright, false smile. "Well, it's only another two weeks to the Easter holidays, so you're not missing much, and then there's the holidays themselves, to help you settle in. And then Thomas told me that one of the women here homeschooled her son."

Jenny folded her arms. "That sounds just fantastic, but you're not homeschooling me, if that's what you think. What do the other kids do?" Pamela didn't answer. Jenny sighed. "There aren't any, are there?"

"There's one. A boy, a bit older."

"Oh, great."

"I'm sure there'll be a nearby school for you. We'll check over the next few days, I promise."

Jenny stepped nearer to her mother, her anger so close to boiling over. "*We'll check over the next few days?* You mean you haven't already, Mum? You dragged us all the way up here, not even bothering to see if there's a school nearby. How will I keep up with my studies and get a job, huh?"

Pamela walked into the kitchen and started to unpack a bag of groceries on the counter. "Honestly, Jenny, most kids hate going to school. They'd be grateful for some time off exams and all that stuff."

Jenny went to stand on the other side of the counter, glaring at her mother. "What about my friends? What about *my* life, Mum? Did you even think about that?"

Pamela met her gaze levelly. "I thought you'd like *this* life. You're always saying how you hate the city. You love going to visit Grandma, and she lives in a tiny village in Scotland."

"Yes. Village. With normal people. And shops. And a

pub. And bloody mobile reception. This isn't a village, Mum!" Jenny's voice had risen steadily, so that she'd ended by practically shouting in her mother's face. Now she took a step back, trying to wind her rage in.

An awkward silence stretched between them. Jenny walked to the window and looked out. There was nothing to see but trees.

Idyllic, she thought bitterly.

"Thomas said that everyone was meeting in the main hall to share the evening meal," Pamela said. "I think it's nice that they all eat together, don't you?"

Jenny neither answered nor turned round.

"Well, I brought some pasta with me. You can eat here tonight if you don't feel up to mixing with anyone."

"And just how am I supposed to cook the pasta? On the log fire?"

Pamela sighed. "I told you, they have electricity here, enough power for basic things, if you don't go crazy and leave the TV on all night. Now, I'm going to be neighbourly. I'll see you later."

Jenny heard the front door close but didn't turn round. She stared out at the dense foliage, concentrating on forcing out her anger one exhalation at a time until her fury had drained away. Then she slumped down on the couch. It was surprisingly comfortable and that irritated her. She could feel the desperately dull future her mother had planned for them wrapping around her; she could sense that her resignation was only a short way off, that she'd find herself suffering through this as she'd suffered through her mother's army of ill-advised boyfriends, just praying this latest fad would end soon.

No. I won't. I'm going to leave here as soon as I can.

Desperate for a distraction from the encroaching

despondency she felt, Jenny went to explore what lay beyond the three doors leading off the main part of the lodge. They led to a main double bedroom, a cramped bathroom, and what was clearly supposed to be a second bedroom, but was carpeted with leaf litter and contained only bare bed frames.

Guess Mum and I are sharing then. Jenny gave a sardonic smile. *At least she won't be jumping into bed with any men if she has to share with me.*

Jenny hauled her suitcase into the usable bedroom. It had a double bed, fitted wardrobe, a chest of drawers and two bedside tables, both with lamps. One table had a battered landline phone on it. She picked up the receiver and heard a dial tone.

That's something, I suppose.

She hefted her suitcase onto the bed and stared at it. She wondered what had happened to all the stuff she'd left behind in their flat. Her mother had told her they'd be staying at her grandmother's house for several weeks and to pack all that was important to her. *I hope that doesn't mean she's just binned everything else.*

No. Mum's stupid, thoughtless, but not cruel. She'd not do that.

Jenny started unpacking. She lay her toiletries on her side of the bed, then set about putting her clothes in the wardrobe and claiming the largest drawers of the cabinet.

As she worked, the evening drew on and the room got darker. She went to the window, preparing to draw the curtains so she could turn on the light. She glanced idly out, her thoughts somewhere else — and a face in the bracken instantly drew her gaze. It disappeared just as she looked directly at it; she'd had only a moment to see it, but even then, she had been filled with a sense of wrongness.

The face had looked human and yet not; the nose was too flat, the eyes too large and the skin more the colour of grey lichen than healthy human skin. She pressed her face against the glass, peering out. Everything was still and undisturbed; doubt filled her mind as to what she'd really seen.

Maybe it's that other kid Mum mentioned. Maybe he thought he'd give the newbies a scare.

Yet her hands shook as she drew the curtains.

This is a shitty place.

She finished unpacking, stashed her suitcase under the bed and then checked her phone. Still no signal.

This is a really shitty place.

CHAPTER THREE

For a few blissful moments when she woke up the next morning, Jenny couldn't remember where she was. Then it all came flooding back and she rolled over with a groan.

"You're awake then," called her mother from the kitchen. She came through, beaming. "I slept wonderfully. What about you?"

"Very badly," Jenny muttered as she swung her legs over the edge of the bed. "There was some wild creature scrabbling around outside."

"Oh! Perhaps a fox. How delightful!"

Jenny tried to hold back a scowl. "Is the shower working?"

"Everything works, dear, I told you."

"Then I'm going to have a shower. A *very* hot one."

"Okay. Shall I wait for you so we can go to breakfast in the main hut together?" There was an almost pleading look to her mother's eyes.

But Jenny's anger was still simmering inside her. "What do you think?"

Pamela's shoulders slumped slightly. "All right, but you *will* have to join in eventually, Jennifer."

So many responses went through her head but Jenny held them in check. She settled for a brittle smile. "Say good morning to Thomas for me."

Pamela beamed. "Of course."

She has, she's fallen under that creepy old bastard's spell, Jenny thought as her mother walked back into the main living quarters.

Jenny grabbed her toiletries bag and a towel that had been in the cupboard when they arrived. Barefoot, she padded through to the bathroom. It might have been cramped and aged, but at least it was clean. Jenny was grudgingly grateful for that; soap scum made her want to puke.

She turned on the shower and was surprised when a powerful blast of water came out. She adjusted the temperature and stepped into the flow. The hot water felt deliciously good against her skin. She tipped her head back, letting it run through her hair. She closed her eyes, as the tension in her head and shoulders began to ease.

She felt water lapping at her feet. A blocked drain meant the hot water had nowhere to go. Her good mood vanished in an instant.

She shuddered, thinking about all the filth sloshing back along the pipes into the base of the shower and onto her skin. She set to washing herself as quickly as possible.

Dan wiped his hands on a tea-towel and said, "I'm going out tonight, Mum."

Selena, his mother, looked over her reading glasses at him, her greying hair falling over her eyes somewhat. "Oh, yes? Are you going round to see the new people? I hear the girl is almost the same age as you. Shame she hasn't turned up to any meals yet."

"No. I'm going on Mick's rounds with him. Just to get some fresh air."

"Oh. Well, okay then."

An hour later, his mother went to bed just as Dan was heading out, a torch in his hand. The sky was clear and filled with stars, the air bitingly cold. The solar streetlights lining the main road clicked on as he passed their motion sensors. He arrived at the gatehouse by the main entrance and knocked on the door.

Mick opened it, shrugging into his own large coat. He looked momentarily surprised to see Dan on his doorstep, then he grinned. "Ah. Company. I'll need a bigger hip flask."

"No, really it's..."

But Mick was already out of earshot.

Drinking. Out late with the most disreputable individual in Haven. This is me, living the high life.

Mick returned and closed the door behind him.

"Aren't we taking Apollo?"

"Not tonight. He's old. The cold gets into his bones. Besides," Mick slapped Dan on the shoulder, "you can be my watchdog tonight."

Dan gave an anxious smile. Having the Alsatian with them would have lessened his nerves. Too many strange things had happened recently to make him completely comfortable with this jaunt.

As they walked the night-watchman's round, the forest was full of nocturnal sounds. The leaves whispered in the breeze, water dripped into unseen pools and creatures scurried through the undergrowth.

"I hate nights like this," Mick grumbled. "The forest is too bloody noisy, you can't do the round properly." A fox in the distance barked. "Shut up, will you?"

Dan grinned, despite his jitteriness. "Have you always been this cantankerous?"

"Yes."

They dodged around two large potholes in the road.

"When's High and Mighty gonna get this fixed? It's a bloody disgrace." Mick winked at Dan. "One good thing about this round is that out here you can say whatever you like. It really lifts your mood. You have to be so careful what you say around Haven. If you offend anyone, there's nowhere to go while things blow over. The nearest pub's over five miles away, and even if you did go and drown your sins, you'd still have to wake up the next morning and face those you'd offended over breakfast. Not to mention still having to carry out your day's work with a hangover."

"You sound like you speak from experience," Dan said.

Mick snorted.

The two of them fell into silence as they turned off the main road down a side road to a collection of lodges. They made a circuit of the clearing, checking the doors and windows of the empty lodges, before heading onto the next clearing.

As he was checking the lock of Holly Lodge, Mick said without turning, "When did you first know?"

Dan froze. *He wants me to talk about it.*

But I'm not ready.

Then why the hell did I come out here? I knew he was going to ask about it. I should have stayed away if I didn't want to.

"You don't have to— Mick began.

But Dan cut him off, the words tumbling unexpectedly out of him. "I thought it was just because there weren't any girls around for me to fancy." He paused, uncertain whether he should continue.

Mick was checking the windows now. "Uh huh." Somehow he managed to imbue those two sounds with sympathy and understanding.

As they went to check the back of the lodge, Dan said, "But then I went into town and I was looking in a clothes shop, and I realised I wasn't looking at the clothes — I was looking at the male dummies, imagining what they'd look like if they were alive. And after that, it was like..."

"Like a floodgate opened?"

"Yes! Exactly. I was looking at men all the time, and I stopped thinking about Selena Gomez when I, you know..."

"When you knocked one out?"

Dan winced. "Yeah. And I started thinking about... guys."

"I was always a fan of Clint Eastwood," Mick said, facing him for the first time.

Dan stared. "That old wrinkly guy?"

"I'm an old wrinkly guy," Mick said with annoyance. He sniffed. "Anyway, he didn't always look like that. I used to dream we were both out there in the desert, alone, nobody to judge."

As they walked back to the main road, Dan said quietly, "I don't think Anna wouldn't like it if she found out. Thomas wouldn't either."

"Fuck Anna and fuck Thomas. Not that I would, of course. One's a girl and the other's a smarmy old git."

Dan laughed, the tension between his shoulders dissolving. It felt good to talk to someone about this.

"Thanks, Mick. It's been on my mind for ages."

"Well, I'm always here. But if you'll take my advice, wait until you've got an escape route from this place before you tell anyone else. I don't think people should hide that part of their nature, but there's a time and a place."

"But you're here. Everybody knows about you. Well, they guess, anyway," he amended, "and nobody minds."

"That's because I'm old, set in my ways, and nobody, male or female, would sleep with me. So they leave me alone. Any abuse that is cast my way, I just ignore it. But you, you're," he sucked his teeth, contemplating, "less robust than me. I think you'd take stuff to heart that I would just brush off."

They had returned to the main gates again. Dan glanced at his watch. Eleven thirty. Mick leant against the wooden gate and took a deep drink from his hip flask before offering it to Dan — who accepted. The whisky burned his throat and quickly warmed his belly.

Dan leant against the gate beside Mick. The road stretched ahead of them, ending with the fountain and the main hut beyond, both lit by moonlight. Surrounding everything were trees, silent black sentinels. Right then, everything was quiet except for the steady drip of water somewhere.

A shriek made them jump. It had sounded so alien to Dan's ears that one question instantly came to mind.

"Is it the witch?"

"Don't be ridiculous. It was just a fox," Mick said, but he didn't sound convinced. He turned his flashlight towards the service path that led down into the forest. "There's something spooking the chickens."

Another shriek sounded, but this time it was closer to a squawk. The bleat of an unhappy goat drifted on the air.

"Come on," Mick said grimly.

The service road led down a slope to a clearing with small animal enclosures. The sounds of dripping water seemed louder now that Dan was among the trees. A light wind had sprung up, making the leaves rustle as if the forest was whispering around him.

Dan's heart was racing as they approached the chicken house and goat pen. His mind populated the shadows with forms that couldn't possibly be there. The chickens were clucking unhappily inside their coop, but the sound was nothing like the terrified squawking Mick and Dan had just heard.

The two of them stood with their backs against the chicken house. They shone their torch beams from left to right. The forest was dark and still.

"It's gone, whatever it was," Mick said quietly.

Something moving underneath the chicken house brushed against Dan's ankle. He cried out and backed away.

"What is it?" Mick asked, retreating too.

Dan stared at the space beneath the chicken house. He expected to see eyes peering back at him, or the slavering snout of a beast.

"Something moved, under there," he said.

"We'll look together, agreed?"

Dan nodded.

"One. Two. Three."

With his heartbeat loud in his ears, Dan crouched down and shone his beam under the chicken house.

There was nothing there.

They straightened up, Dan fighting down his panic.

"You wait here," Mick said, "I'll do a circuit."

As Mick moved off, Dan felt at a loss. He didn't want his back towards the henhouse again, but facing away from the looming trees felt just as exposed.

As Mick did two slow loops of the animal pens, Dan turned on the spot, trying to shine his torch everywhere at once. He could hear the smacking of the goats' lips as they chewed the cud. The chickens had gone quiet.

He saw that there were scratches on the chicken house door, some old ones on the door itself and new ones around the padlock. Dan swallowed, wishing he had more whisky. The undergrowth behind him rustled and he spun round, but nothing emerged.

"See anything?" Mick asked, approaching him.

"No. I thought so but... no."

"Let's go. The animals are safe, and I want my bed."

Dan nodded his agreement, and the two of them turned and walked back up the service road as quickly as they could.

CHAPTER FOUR

Jenny was sitting on her bed reading when her mother marched in and declared, "Jennifer Pine, you are coming to lunch with me."

Jenny thought of the plastic bag under the bed; she'd stockpiled the small amount of food she'd brought for the car journey, but all that was left was a third of a packet of prawn cocktail crisps. Her stomach rumbled.

Jenny sighed and stood up. "Yeah, okay then."

Pamela looked startled. "Oh. Good. Everybody's curious about you."

"Great," Jenny said, without much feeling.

Stepping outside for the first time since their arrival, Jenny was struck by the silence that surrounded her. She'd always been used to the background hum of city life; even in her grandmother's village, there were still the distant sounds of cars or tractors and sheep in distant fields. Here there was only the wind soughing through the leaves. It was eerie. She felt that if she uttered a sound it would be swallowed by the trees around her.

The main hut had a room that had clearly been intended as a restaurant for the holiday park; at the far end was a service hatch into the kitchen beyond. Three long tables with benches attached stretched the length of the room, even though Jenny could see only about a dozen people. A small, petite woman in her late thirties was passing food through the hatch while two elderly women trotted to and fro, laying out the food on another long table set against the wall.

"There's a rota," Pamela informed her as they helped themselves to food, "so that everyone has a turn at cooking meals. Isn't that fantastic?"

The food was simple but tasty: home-baked bread, goats cheese that was so strong Jenny could only eat a small amount, potato salad, some smoked ham, some pickles and a sweet berry cordial. She tried to focus on eating as her mother showed her off to everyone. Jenny smiled politely, shook hands when necessary, exchanged small talk when prompted, and tried to disguise her unease.

Where are all the black people? she thought as she scanned the room. *Where are all the kids? The young families? It feels more like some kind of exclusive, white middle-aged club than a proper community.*

Despite her discomfort, she took an instant liking to Mick, 'the security dosser' as he introduced himself. He winked. "At my age, I'm due a bit of dossing." His handshake was firm, his hand rough with calluses but warm.

He asked her how she was settling in, then made a joke about Thomas that nearly caused Jenny to spit her mouthful of bread across the table. Pamela scowled but said nothing. Mick then proceeded to tell them a few stories about his life before Haven that had Pamela's eyes nearly popping out of their sockets with their lewdness.

Eventually, it got too much for her. "Maybe you had best grab a bite of lunch, Mick. I haven't seen you eat anything yet and they'll be clearing away soon."

Mick's expression became serious. "You're quite right, love, and how kind of you to notice. I'll leave you be, but you and the lass are always welcome at mine for a drink or whatever."

Pamela shifted uncomfortably. "That's kind of you

and—"

"And if you pop round I'll even let you stroke my doggy," Mick added with a suggestive smile.

Pamela stiffened, uncertainty and horror written all over her face. Jenny let out a loud, brash laugh.

"What?" Mick asked innocently. "My Apollo's lovely and such a well behaved Alsatian." He gave Jenny a conspiratorial grin before heading to the food table.

"I don't think he's very funny," said Pamela archly once he was out of earshot. Her cheeks had spots of red on them.

Jenny grinned. "I do."

"You would."

Mick was definitely the highlight of lunch, but Jenny found most of the residents she met to be reasonably friendly. The two elderly women she'd seen ferrying food turned out to be sisters, Millicent and Esme. They looked like they'd just stepped out of a film from the 1950s. They were both quite short, finished each other's sentences, and wore perpetual smiles and thick spectacles. They were falling over themselves to be welcoming: Esme measured Jenny up for a thick woollen sweater she promised to knit, while Millicent said she'd bring round a blanket they'd crocheted last year which could be used as a bedspread.

Then there was Eustace whose skill was carpentry. He was so softly spoken, Jenny had to strain to catch what he was saying at times. When he told them that he ran several part-time woodworking classes at a nearby college, Jenny wondered how on earth his students could hear him over the sounds of saws and machinery. She also met a couple called David and Andrea. David was an ex-supermarket manager who had contacts within the food industry. When he wasn't working at Haven, he'd travel round to farmer's markets and craft fairs, trying to sell the produce from Haven. Andrea was the woman who'd be serving behind the hatch. She used to work at a garden centre and she had a job one day a week at a florist in a nearby town.

Finally there was Selena and Dan, the latter being the 'other kid' that Pamela had spoken of. Selena had black hair peppered with plenty of grey and a warm smile. She had a degree in languages and taught distance-learning courses. She was desperate to pass onto them a host of recipes that they might need. In contrast, Dan was awkward and quiet, as if he was trying to find an excuse to get away from them all. That didn't stop his mother singing his praises though.

"Yes, he's quite the handyman," she concluded after telling them about the maintenance work he was currently undertaking on the generators, "truly indispensable to the community. I'm hoping one day he might take an engineering degree or something. Then he could return and teach us everything he knows."

Come back? Jenny thought. *I don't think I would if I managed to escape this place.* But since everyone had been so nice, she kept her thoughts to herself.

With what she hoped was a sweet smile, she asked, "So, how long have you been here, Dan?"

"Since I was ten. Excuse me." Dan bobbed his head in goodbye then hurried off to join Mick at a different table.

Selena reddened and cleared her throat. "He's a strange one, but sweet. Ever so sweet." She gave Jenny a look laced with meaning; Jenny glanced at Pamela and found the look mirrored on her face.

Shit. They've betrothed us already.

Her thoughts were broken by the arrival of Thomas, Anna, and a man they introduced as Samuel Harrison. He was a trained pharmacist and a sort of informal doctor for Haven. He had dark, greasy hair, wonky teeth and a habit of not meeting your eyes when he spoke. Jenny hoped it was shyness and not just Samuel staring at her breasts while he talked to her. Anna very proudly informed them that Samuel was the grandson of one of their founders and therefore had a very special role in Haven. "He and I drew up the rules together, you know," Anna said, with a meaningful look at Pamela and Jenny.

There are rules? That can't be good.

"So how are you settling in?" Thomas asked.

"Brilliantly, thank you," Pamela replied.

"Good, good. I hope you like it in Ash Lodge. It's a lovely little place."

"Despite its history," Anna said coldly.

There was an awkward silence around the table. Jenny exchanged a look with Pamela who asked, "History?"

"It's nothing," said Thomas. He glared at his wife who ignored him.

"A slut lived there once," Anna informed them. She smiled at Pamela. It was a cold, cruel smile. "That woman only came here to cause trouble. She was a tart: dressed as such, acted as such."

Thomas opened his mouth, but Anna marched on. "We're a good, honest establishment here and she worked to tear our little family apart. We asked her to leave and it was the best decision we made in some time. She was not suitable for Haven. Those kind of people never are."

"Oh," said Pamela uncertainly. "Would it help if we moved to a different lodge? We don't want to be associated with troublemakers."

"None of the others are prepared," Anna said curtly.

"But if the lodge is not to your liking," Thomas

interjected, "then I'm sure other arrangements could be made." He and Anna glared at each other; Anna looked away first.

"Well, I think it will be brilliant for you to stay there," Samuel said. He'd been staring at Pamela in earnest; but, as every eye turned towards him, his gaze dropped back to his plate. "I mean, it'll help clean away the bad memories by having two good people living in the place."

"Exactly," Thomas said decisively. "After all, the woman my wife mentioned has been gone almost a decade now. It's old history."

"A decade?" Jenny asked. "Why hasn't anyone lived in Ash Lodge since then?" She noticed the discomfort her question caused and sensed that there was more to the history of this previous occupant than they'd been told.

"The place needed quite some renovation. Now, please excuse me," Thomas said brusquely. He stood up and left. Jenny had expected Anna to follow him, but she merely sat there, staring at Jenny and her mother.

Something tells me this isn't finished yet.
Well, bring it on.

Dan kept his head down as Thomas left the room. Mick gave a cackle as he got out his cigarette papers and tobacco tin. "Quite fitting, don't you think? Anna putting them in that lodge."

Dan felt a chill grip his stomach. "Why?"

"Well, it's clear Thomas has a thing for that Pamela. And you can tell from the way she looks at him that he's half the reason she's here."

Dan sighed. "What is it about that man? It's not like he's good-looking."

"Oh, I don't know," mused Mick, filling a flattened

paper with tobacco, "he has a certain presence about him."

Dan looked at the gatekeeper askance.

Mick winked. "But still a smarmy old git."

Anna's raised voice caused Dan, and everyone else, to look at the newcomers. "Yes, a very strict moral code, young lady. Some of us believe they are standards for living dictated by God, while even those who don't believe in Him," Dan detected the familiar disdain in her voice, "still agree that the Code contains rules suitable for community living."

"Oh yeah? And what exactly in this Code?" Jenny asked, meeting Anna's glare with one of her own. Dan was impressed; most people, himself included, wilted under that woman's stare.

Anna straightened, preparing to deliver a familiar sermon. "Firstly, there shall be no theft of other people's belongings."

"Glad to know my stuff will be safe," Jenny said coldly.

"Secondly, there shall be no falsehoods spoken on matters of import. Thirdly, relationships shall be between men and women only, none of the... other kind."

Jenny snorted. "Christ! What century are you people living in?"

"Fourthly, there shall be no blaspheming!" Anna practically shouted. She cleared her throat, and resumed in more normal tones. "Fifthly, marriage is sacred. There shall be no relationships outside of marriage." Anna leant forward, a cold glint in her eye. "Such relationships are offensive to all morals."

Jenny stood up; so did Anna. In a cold voice, Jenny said, "Is that so? What about children born of such relationships?"

Dan's eyes flicked to Pamela, who had paled and was staring up at her daughter.

Anna leant forward. "Monstrous," she said, in a whisper that carried the full length of the hall.

Jenny's voice was strained. "Well, I'm glad that's all cleared up."

"Yes, definitely," said Pamela, standing up quickly. "We fully understand those rules and would never dream of breaking them."

Anna glared at Jenny for a few more seconds, then gave a curt nod. She spun on her heel and stalked out of the room. All around the hall, people turned back to their meals and resumed their conversations, though in lower tones than before.

"You know, I think I like that new girl quite a lot," Mick said quietly. "Bit of a temper on her, but that's not always a bad thing."

Dan wasn't really listening. He was thinking of Anna's words, of the disgust they'd contained.

God, she'd hate me if she really knew. Samuel too I bet. Would they cast me out, like a dog? Would Mum let them? He felt wretched and looked down to hide the tears pricking his eyes.

"The rules amuse me," Mick said idly.

Dan looked up sharply. "They do? Why?"

Mick gave him a cruel smile. "Well, it's hard to take anything seriously from a man who had an affair with a witch."

Dan's mouth fell open. "What, with *the* witch?"

Mick chuckled. "I know of only one witch in Haven, so we're likely thinking of the same one. Although I never thought of her as a witch — just an angry, hurt woman."

"What was she like?"

34

"That's a story for another day. Maybe another night-time stroll?"

Dan considered. "Yeah, okay."

"Excellent." Mick got up, taking his empty plate away and leaving Dan with a dozen questions running through his mind.

CHAPTER FIVE

After a day walking round the commune, seeing the turbines and solar panels, meeting the animals, learning about all the different tasks that had to be done, Jenny was exhausted. And as her exhaustion grew, so did her anger at having all this change thrust upon her until she was just as furious as she had been that first night.

As the day darkened to evening outside, Jenny stood in Ash Lodge, her arms folded. "I don't care, Mum. I'm not staying."

Pamela clenched her fists, a rare sign of anger. "But you haven't given it a chance. We've barely been here a day."

"I don't care, Mum. I'm not staying."

"Stop saying that!" Pamela yelled.

Jenny was taken aback. Her mother was normally so docile, so eager to please; it was unlike her to raise her voice.

I guess I've really gone too far this time. She wasn't even that angry when I signed up for the pole dancing lessons.

But this isn't my fault. She dragged me here.

Pamela drew a deep breath and exhaled slowly. "I know things haven't been easy on you, Jenny. I ask a lot of you, what with changing jobs all the time—"

"And changing boyfriends." It was a cheap shot, and Jenny felt bad when her mother winced.

"But I really think this will be good for us. If you're worried about your studies, then I spoke to Anna and she said that there's a school a forty minute bus ride away. There's a bus stop on the main road."

"And what about my friends? The projects I was working on at my old school? What about my life back home?"

"How about you act like a grown-up, Jennifer, and learn to deal with the hand life deals you?"

"And how about you act like my mother and try to think what's best for me, rather than you, for a change?" Jenny retorted. Her mother winced again, but this time Jenny felt no remorse.

"I can see we're not going to resolve this tonight," said Pamela archly. "I don't know what else to say, so I'm going to bed. Goodnight."

Jenny turned away, not dignifying her mother with an answer. She heard soft footsteps, then the bathroom door open and close. Jenny sat on the couch, waiting for Pamela to come out of the bathroom and apologise. But when her mother was finished, Pamela merely walked wordlessly to the bedroom and closed the door.

Jenny fumed for fifteen minutes, after which she felt even more mentally and physically exhausted than before. She went to the window and opened it wide. She'd been expecting a blast of fresh air, but what hit her instead was the stink of ammonia.

Jenny reeled back, her hand going up to her mouth. In the light from the window, she saw a patch of bracken beneath the trees swaying slightly. As she watched, it gradually stilled.

Was that the wind? Or was someone there? A fox maybe, or a deer. Must have been an animal, with a stink like that.

She shuddered and closed the window.

I've got to get out of here. The thought arrived in her head with such force and conviction that it took her by surprise. She mulled it over. *I could go home. It's still the weekend so I haven't missed any school yet. If I can't get into our old flat, I could sleep on Amy's couch. She wouldn't mind. I could call Gran, explain how stupid Mum's been. I bet Gran would lend me some money, or come down and stay with me.*

But what about Mum? Yeah, she's a shit mother, but she's still my mum. I'd be leaving her here, on her own, with that creep Thomas.

She'll be fine. After all, she wanted to come. She'll stay here a few weeks, maybe a month or so, get bored of this fad like all the others, then she'll come home. She'll be grateful to me for keeping our old life in the city going. Yeah, it'll be me that was right and she'll have to acknowledge it.

Jenny grinned at the thought. She opened the door to the bedroom and tiptoed inside. She quietly retrieved her bag from under the bed and repacked her clothes. She grabbed her toiletries from the bathroom, then put on her coat. Forcing down the guilt she felt, Jenny reached inside Pamela's coat, drew out her purse, and stuffed all the notes from there into her pocket.

She paused at the doorway, guilt again tugging at her heartstrings. She glanced round once, then stepped out into the night.

Her first thought was to find the bus stop her mother had mentioned. But as she walked along the central road, she saw that the main gates had been closed. They were padlocked as well. Jenny bit her lip and glanced at the gatekeeper's lodge. The downstairs lights were on.

I could ask Mick for the key. Would he give it to me?

Would he let me out, or would he call for Mum?

She stood there, uncertain. Around her, the forest was silent, as if holding its breath, waiting for her decision.

No, he'd call for Mum. I'll have to find my own way out.

She turned to her left and followed a service road into the wood. A few steps in and she realised she couldn't see anything. The main road had streetlights on motion sensors, but none of that illumination filtered into the forest.

Bloody hell, it's dark. She swallowed around the lump in her throat and fished out her phone. She switched on the torch. The meagre light didn't help much; only the nearest trees and patches of undergrowth were visible. Rather than comforting her, it made the darkness beyond its paltry beam seem even more sinister.

Jenny pulled her coat tighter. It was colder beneath the trees and her breath steamed in front of her. She hurried on, more eager than ever to be gone from this strange place.

She hadn't travelled far when she found that the service road ended with a collection of animal shelters. The air bore the odour of fresh hay and warm bodies. She thought of the ammonia she'd smelled from outside her window and sniffed experimentally. There was no trace of it here.

She turned and headed back towards the main road, cursing under her breath at this setback. She slowed as she drew closer; she didn't want to be seen by anyone who might go and wake Pamela. But the road was deserted.

She walked past Mick's house and started along a gravel path which led up a slight incline. She quickly switched to walking on the verge instead, the crunch of gravel too loud in the oppressive silence. When she crested the top of the slope, she laughed with relief. Below her was a car park with a road beyond winding through the forest. There were only about half a dozen vehicles, spaced out in a rectangle of tarmac meant for twenty. There were two hatchbacks, a battered estate, Pamela's five door, a Land Rover, and a Discovery caked in mud with a trailer next to it. It was a patch of the modern world amongst nature and her joy at the sight only confirmed how much she needed to leave Haven.

She hurried down the incline and started across the car park towards the winding road. Floodlights came on, dazzling her and she held her hand up to shield her eyes from the sudden brightness.

Is everything around her on a bloody motion sensor?

She looked around nervously, her gaze drawn to the trees around the car park.

I can't see anything out there.

But anything out there could see me.

Suddenly being in a well-lit area surrounded by darkness made her feel even more vulnerable.

A scuffling from behind the Land Rover made her pulse jump. Every muscle in her body went rigid. It was an effort to force her head that way to look. Jenny stood still for several minutes, but there was no further noise. She let out a shaky exhalation and walked on. The scuffling started up again and she stopped. It stopped too.

Breathing hard now, she walked faster across the tarmac. She fixed her eyes on the road that wound off into the trees, desperate to put the car park behind her. The floodlight to her left started flickering. She sped up.

Jenny was about ten feet from the road when a dark shape raced across it. She registered a long, thin body running on all fours, before it vanished from sight into the undergrowth. Jenny spun round, intending to run back across the car park, maybe even all the way back to Ash Lodge. But all the lights behind her had gone out. Only the one next to her was on. It started to flicker.

The scuffling noise came from behind the trailer next to her. It was accompanied by the sound of wet, rasping breathing.

Pressure was growing within Jenny's chest, as if iron bars were squeezing her tight. She saw movement on the other side of the trailer, just as the last remaining floodlight began to flicker. She tried to hold onto the belief that what she was hearing was only a fox or a cat and that she'd laugh at her own stupidity when it ran out in front of her. But such thoughts were mere drops in the ocean of her terror. She stepped backwards, cursing the crunch of stones that betrayed her movements.

A shadow rose from behind the trailer, much taller than a cat or a fox. It was in silhouette, only its hunched outline was visible and its features indistinguishable in the growing darkness. It was human shaped, but wrong: the arms were too long, the head not quite the right shape. It sniffed at the air.

The floodlight went off and Jenny cried out. She fled towards the road through the trees, desperate to be anywhere but here. Her bag bounced painfully against her hip; her lungs felt on fire as she dragged in cold air. She stumbled once, and again, but she kept going.

A figure stepped out ahead of her. Jenny cannoned into it, screaming as arms snaked around her waist and held her tightly.

"Let me go!" she screamed, wriggling and thrashing. "Let me go!" But the arms only gripped her tighter.

CHAPTER SIX

"Jenny! It's me, Dan. Stop screaming!"

His words finally penetrated her panic and she stilled. She peered up at him.

"D-Dan?"

"Yes. Who did you think it was?"

"I... I don't know. There was someone, in the car park."

"Someone?"

"Yeah. Or... something. I — I don't know." She was trembling.

"Do you want me to go and check what's back there?" he asked.

Please say no.

She gave him a weak smile. "No. Just stay here with me for a bit, until I calm down, if that's okay?"

"Yeah. Sure." In an effort to hide his relief, he bent to pick up his torch, which he'd dropped when she'd crashed into him.

She frowned, suspicion creeping into her eyes. "What are you doing out here anyway?"

"I'm helping Mick with his rounds. I've just walked down to check on the gate to the main road. Sometimes drivers get lost, open the gate to turn round then drive off without shutting it."

"And was it open?" Her voice was strained; he guessed she wanted mundane conversation to take her mind off whatever she'd encountered.

"No." He shuffled his feet, feeling uncomfortable. "Look, I've got to get back. Would it make you feel better if we walked through the car park together? Watching out for each other?"

Please say yes.

Jenny glanced over her shoulder, biting her bottom lip. "Sure. That sounds great."

As they made their way back along the path, Jenny walked so close that her coat sleeve brushed against him. Dan moved a little way from her and said, "You know, Thomas thinks there's teenage vandals around, leaving scratches on doors, sneaking around in Halloween masks. Maybe it's one of them you saw."

Jenny frowned. "Maybe. But it was weird. It looked human-shaped, but wrong as well. It sniffed the air like an animal. And there was this intense pressure in my chest, almost as if..." She shook her head. "Probably just me being stupidly afraid. The bloody lights didn't help either. You need to fix them." She looked at him curiously. "Do you think it might have seen a kid messing around in the car park?"

No. The answer arrived in his head without any conscious deliberation.

He ran his fingers through his hair. "I don't know. Some stuff has happened to other people: me, Mick, Millicent. She thought she saw a monster's face at the window one night when she was doing the washing up. Mick's found... stuff, and I've felt watched from the woods at times. Thomas claims it's teenagers, and he might be right, but somehow everything that's happened feels more... sinister." He paused. She nodded and he was encouraged to go on. "I mean, Mick found this rabbit. It had been killed, taken apart carefully then laid out, like an experiment. Seems a bit brutal and pointless for kids."

"Maybe psycho kids."

"Maybe." That theory didn't make him feel any better. He gave a bitter laugh. "I'm just waiting for Anna or Samuel to tell us all that it's a punishment from God for some sin we've committed."

"Oh yeah? Committed any sins recently, Dan?"

Dan stared at her, uncertain if she was serious or mocking him.

She grinned and nudged him. "I was just teasing. Don't look so worried. I need to know you another twenty-four hours before I expect you to tell me all your deepest darkest secrets."

Dan laughed, feeling the tension ease slightly. Jenny glanced ahead of them and stopped. They were at the edge of the car park. She pointed at the Land Rover. "Whatever was stalking me hid over there."

Dan's mouth went dry. "Do you want to go and look? See if it's still there? Or shall we just get the hell away from this place?"

"Let's get the hell away," Jenny replied, gripping his arm tightly. They set off across the car park, the lights flicking on as they passed by the sensor. The illumination made Dan feel strangely vulnerable.

It's because there are shadows around the edges, he thought, glancing anxiously at the dark trees. *We're in the middle of a bubble of light, and the darkness is pressing in on all sides.* He picked up the pace; Jenny matched him.

There was a rustling in the undergrowth to their right. They exchanged a nervous look before hurrying on. Jenny's pace became so fast she was almost jogging and, since she was still gripping his arm, Dan was forced to keep apace. He kept glancing to the right, certain that he saw something darting among the trees.

"You feel that?" Jenny asked. She tapped her chest. "The pressure, in there?"

Dan did. He felt as if invisible hands were pushing him backwards.

"It's just panic," he said, although even he didn't think he sounded convincing.

They were most of the way across the car park now. The rustling had stopped and the pressure had eased, but that didn't make Dan feel any better. They were drawing closer to the path that led up the slope, into the trees and towards Haven.

"Big burst of speed up the hill?" Jenny asked, panting a little.

"Yep."

They charged it, but the path was so narrow that they struggled to get up it together, slipping and sliding on the loose stones and dirt. Tension and anticipation grew inside Daniel with each step; the end was in sight, but he had a dreadful premonition that something would jump out of the trees at the last moment before they reached safety.

They stopped at the top of the incline, Dan's legs burning with the effort. A dark shape was coming towards them along the path. Jenny spun round, ready to dart back the way they'd come.

"No! Wait! It's Mick," Dan said, catching hold of her coat.

"Of course it's me," said Mick. "Who'd you think it was?"

Dan looked at Jenny, who stared mutely back. Everything had all seemed so real when they were crossing the car park, but now that he came to vocalise their fears,

Dan wasn't sure whether they weren't just being silly.

"Had an encounter with something, did you?" Mick asked, his gaze flicking between them.

Jenny told him of what had happened. Mick stepped closer to the two of them, his gaze going past their shoulders and scanning the car park beyond.

"Come on," he muttered, "let's get home. There's a bad taste on the wind tonight."

Neither Jenny nor Dan raised any argument and the three of them hurried down the path together. They didn't speak again until they'd reached the brightly lit central road. There they stopped, looked behind them and then at each other, somewhat sheepishly.

It was Jenny who eventually broke the silence. "So, I guess it's not really a good time to join the commune then, what with vandals or possible monsters roaming around."

Dan gave a forced laugh. "Oh, I don't know. You're joining when all the excitement is kicking off."

More seriously, Mick added, "Things aren't great. If you or your mother wanted to leave, no one would blame you."

Jenny's hand went to the bag at her shoulder, the movement drawing Dan's attention to it for the first time — and realisation dawned.

I can't believe I didn't see that before. She was running away.

Jenny looked at the ground, scuffing a stone with her shoe. "My mum won't leave, and what kind of heartless bitch would I be if I ran off and left her with all this crap going on?" She gave a hollow laugh.

Dan wasn't sure what response she was expecting, or if she was expecting any at all, so he followed Mick's lead and kept quiet. She stared at the ground for a few more seconds, lost in her own thoughts, then looked up and gave them both a shy smile.

"I guess I'm your co-conspirator with all these weird goings-on now."

Mick grinned. "Pleasure to have you on board, lass."

"I'd best get back before Mum finds me gone. Night."

Dan felt his heart lift as he watched her walk away. He suddenly realised how sad he would have been if he'd woken up tomorrow to find Jenny gone. Maybe he really did need someone his own age around.

"Nice lass," Mick commented.

"Yeah," said Dan, "she's okay. I like her better when she's not so angry."

CHAPTER SEVEN

Jenny didn't sleep at all well that night. She dreamed of being chased. Jolted awake by her own nightmares at 2 am, she could have sworn she heard scratching at the bedroom window. But when she'd sat up in bed, listening intently, the noise had stopped and hadn't returned.

She'd eventually settled down again and drifted into a light sleep. When her eyes opened again, it was lighter outside and the clock read 07:23. *Everyone else will be going to school this morning. I should have had Maths with Miss. Hove first, then Science with Mr. Phillips but instead I'm stuck here. I won't get to hear how Amy's date with Mark went. I won't get to plan an outfit for the Easter Extravaganza party.* In place of the hot anger she'd felt yesterday, now she felt only a numb resignation. *What awaits me today, I wonder? A day of hard labour? Hoeing onions, milking cows, mucking out horses? All good "hands on experience",* she thought bitterly.

Pamela stirred beside her. Jenny rolled over, watching her mother wake up. *You're the reason I stayed, you know. You're a daft bitch, but I do love you. I couldn't leave you here with all this weird shit going on. I hope you appreciate that.*

Pamela opened her eyes blearily. She stared at the ceiling for a moment before looking at Jenny. Her smile was warm and genuine. "Hello, little chicken. I think the last time you and I shared a bed together was when you were five and having nightmares."

Jenny pulled a face, although she was touched by the use of her mother's old nickname for her. "Yeah, well, don't get used to it. I'm going to speak to Thomas today and insist that he sort out that other room. You snore."

Pamela laughed and Jenny felt her spirits lift. Her mother had looked so worn and weary recently, it was good to see her smile properly.

Pamela reached out, tenderly stroking a strand of hair away from Jenny's face. Quietly she said, "I just want us to get on with life here. I won't mention it again, but before we get up, I want to say thank you for staying, for not leaving last night."

Jenny's breath caught in her throat.

Her surprise must have shown on her face as Pamela added, "This isn't a prison. It's supposed to be a better life, for both of us. But if you want to leave, I won't hold that against you. I told Gran where we are, so just give her a call and she'll help you out. Okay?"

Jenny nodded.

Pamela smiled, and threw back the covers. "Now, since you're here, it's breakfast in the main hut for both of us."

Jenny groaned, but her mother was already up and through the door, leaving no room for argument. Jenny dragged herself reluctantly out of bed, then headed straight for the shower. When she had scrubbed her skin a bright pink and her hair smelled of coconut, she felt more prepared to face the day.

She got dressed then opened the front door and stared out at the forest. There was dew on the grass and a low mist twisted among the trees. Jenny could hear voices in the distance as well as doors opening and closing, as their neighbours went to breakfast. Yet since neither of the other two cabins in the clearing was occupied, Jenny had the sense of being lost in the woods on the outskirts of civilisation. It brought goosebumps to her skin.

A pile of mud and detritus on the porch drew her attention. There were grass stalks with muddy roots, some damp twigs and, underneath, a wilting daffodil. She leant down to examine the heap more closely but instantly straightened up again, as she caught a whiff of pungent ammonia.

"What's that?" asked Pamela, coming up behind her.

"I don't know, but it's disgusting."

"Debris blown here by the wind?"

"I don't think so. Not with all that mud. Plus it looks sort of... arranged." Dan's story about the dead rabbit came back to her and her stomach gave a little flip.

Pamela shrugged. "Clear it away, will you? We don't want to tramp mud into the lodge."

Jenny used the edge of her shoe to push the mud pile off the step. The sight of it lying scattered on the ground filled her with a strange regret that she couldn't quite put her finger on. But then Pamela was ushering her off the porch and she had no further time to think on it.

They were about halfway down the path to the main road when Jenny saw a figure walking towards them. It was Samuel, the pharmacist. When he caught her eye, he smiled and smoothed his greasy hair.

"Good morning to our newest residents," he said brightly. "I thought you might appreciate some company on the way to breakfast."

"Oh, thank you, that would be lovely," replied Pamela. Jenny turned her head away in disgust at the simpering tone in her mother's voice.

As they walked, Samuel chattered away and Pamela

laughed on cue. Jenny paid attention for a little bit, but the way Samuel's eyes kept sliding towards her with a knowing look made her uncomfortable.

Then he surprised her by saying, "So, I guess you'll be working with me today, Jenny. Are you looking forward to it?"

Jenny stared at him in surprise. Pamela looked sheepish. "I hope you don't mind, sweetheart, but I know you wanted to be a vet, and Samuel looks after the animals here—"

"As well as being the resident pharmacist and amateur doctor," Samuel interrupted.

Pamela threw him a small smile. "Yes, a man of many talents. And I thought you might enjoy working with the animals."

Jenny looked from her mother's hopeful expression to the pharmacist who wore a self-satisfied smirk. She forced a smile on her face. "That sounds lovely."

CHAPTER EIGHT

A day spent with the animals was more instructive and enjoyable than Jenny had thought it would be. Samuel was an utter show-off for the first half an hour, but as they got down to the business of mucking out, dishing out food, refilling water troughs, and brushing down and collecting eggs, his manner became more professional and less obnoxious.

Only when they came to milking the goats did she feel really uncomfortable. He sat her on a stool and encouraged her to have a go, but she got it so wrong that the goat bucked and bleated. After that, he insisted on sitting behind her, his arms around her, showing her how to do it. Jenny felt distinctly uncomfortable; his aftershave was overwhelming and the heat of his body pressed against hers made her feel incredibly claustrophobic. Only when he finally stood up did she allow a shudder of revulsion to run through her.

The day sped by and, after they'd shut the animals in for the night, Jenny was exhausted. But she didn't feel like going home just yet. She wanted some fresh air to clear away the scent of Samuel's sweat and aftershave, so she resolved to explore the commune a bit.

She wandered around the back of the main hall and was surprised to find a huge swimming pool, with a domed roof of corrugated plastic. Through the plastic she could make out rows and rows of plants and she realised that she was looking at a greenhouse. A crude square hatch opened at the edge of the roof and Dan's head popped out. He was climbing up the ladder set into the side of the swimming pool. When he saw her, he smiled and waved. Jenny was surprised to find that was enough to wipe away the unpleasantness of the day.

"How've you been?" he asked as she walked over.

"I've been looking after the animals."

"With Samuel?"

"Yes."

"And how did you find that?"

"Instructive."

And uncomfortable.

"I see," he replied, as if he'd read her mental addendum.

"What's down there?" she asked, keen to move the conversation on.

"Haven't you seen it yet? Then let me give you the grand tour! Come on down." He clambered back down the ladder.

Intrigued, Jenny followed. As she descended, she sensed the change in atmosphere: the air was warm and humid. She saw rows of plants, on tables, on the floor, hanging from the ceiling and climbing up the walls.

Dan threw his arms wide. "Welcome to Eden! Everything in here is edible. There's beans, peppers, courgettes, lettuce, and when we have a glut of produce, we store it every way we can think of. One year we had tomato chutney with every meal except breakfast."

"Sounds... lovely."

"Do you like plants?"

"They're okay, but I'm no good with them. I killed a cactus once, and those things are supposed to survive anything." They both laughed.

Dan took her up and down the length of the swimming pool, showing her the hanging baskets full of strawberry plants, the pots of cucumbers and the seedling potatoes in Grobags lining the floor. He showed her the series of pipes and tubes that filtered rain from the domed roof into water butts dotted around the greenhouse. He even showed her his secret stash of sweet pea plants.

"I thought you said everything in here was edible?"

He smiled sheepishly. "They're my weakness. They just smell so beautiful and I love the way one plant can give you so many colours. They don't take up much room. Don't tell anyone, okay?" He looked at her with such shyness that Jenny found herself nodding before she even knew she was doing it.

"I'm good at keeping secrets. You can tell me anything," she said. He looked suddenly uncomfortable and Jenny moved on hurriedly. "Were you always good at gardening?"

"I guess so. My dad was a big gardener, before he left us. After he went, I kind of kept it up. When Mum started the process of moving here, I put it down as a strength on my application and then was surprised at how much I remembered. Have you met Andrea? She managed a garden centre for years and now works part-time at a florist, so she's much better than me at all this stuff. I try to work with her whenever I can and learn anything she teaches me."

As Dan picked up a watering can and started to water the potatoes, Jenny frowned in thought. "Andrea. She's the one that lives with David, isn't she?"

"Yep."

"Someone told me they're ex-husband and wife."

"That's right. It's... difficult in Haven if you want to split up with your partner. We're such a close community, it could cause a lot of discomfort and upset. If you leave, you take your specialist skills with you and it might be some time before the community can replace you. But if you stay..."

Jenny could imagine the uncomfortable atmosphere. "You would have thought that at least one of them could have moved out."

"When they split up, all the habitable lodges were taken. Then, when one did become available, it looked like they'd reached some kind of understanding. Now they seem perfectly happy with the arrangement."

"It all sounds complicated — and like a gun primed to go off."

"Maybe, but it seems to work, for them anyway. This place offers a lot of opportunities, if you abide by the rules." He spoke with a touch of bitterness.

"You mean the Code that Anna was talking about?"

Dan nodded. "Most of the rules are just common sense, like what to do once the gates close. But unfortunately, Anna and Samuel have seen to it that some are a bit... stricter."

"And what about Thomas and his wandering eye? How does *he* cope with the moral stuff?" Dan looked at her with surprise and she snorted a laugh. "Come on. I've seen the way he looks at my mother, looks at me even."

Dan shrugged. "He's a reformed character, apparently. There was a load of strife at his old workplace. He was a lecturer at a university, and the female students made so many complaints against him that he was forced to leave. Anna used to be his secretary, you know."

Jenny thought of the acidic looks the woman had shot

at Pamela. "Explains a lot."

Dan stepped closer. Jenny found herself leaning towards him.

"Mick told me that when Samuel arrived, he and Anna sort of joined forces on the moral front. Samuel's the grandson of one of the founding members, so he carries quite some weight here. The Code was already in place for sensible things, but Anna and Samuel added to it. That's why there's only a few old-timers here. Everyone who was younger moved away pretty quickly. The way Mick tells it, the rules on extra-marital affairs were included by Anna specifically to deal with her husband."

"And does he abide by them?"

"Yes, he does," said a cold voice behind them. Jenny turned. Anna was standing there, her arms crossed and her cheeks red. She glared at Dan, then took a step towards Jenny.

"My husband, as that young man put it, is now a reformed character."

Jenny swallowed nervously. *Shit. If she heard that, she's heard all the rest.* She glanced at Dan, who was decidedly pale.

"He now understands the mortal sin of having an affair. It is a filthy failing and any children born of such unions will undoubtedly grow up to be monstrous."

Jenny bridled, clenching her fists. "Yes, Anna. You've already made your feelings on that point very clear."

"The sins of the father are passed onto the children," Anna quoted piously. Then a cruel gleam came into her eyes and her lips pulled into an ugly smile. "Do you think that's true, Jennifer? Oh wait, I'm sorry. I asked the wrong question. I should have perhaps started with asking if you actually knew *who* your father was in the first place."

Jenny felt rooted to the spot, her fury incapacitating her. It surged through her, only just under control. She knew if she opened her mouth she would spit out curses; if she moved at all, it would be to swing her arm back and punch this woman in her smug face.

Anna nodded in satisfaction. "I thought so. You and your mother look just the types."

Jenny took a step closer to the smirking woman and said in a low voice, "You know nothing about us."

Anna met her gaze levelly and whispered, "Monstrous."

The edges of the world seemed to blur. Jenny struggled to draw a full breath in the heat and humidity. Jenny knew anger was her weakness, and she wasn't going to show weakness to Anna, no matter how much the woman taunted her.

Anna turned to Dan and sneered. "And you, young man, spend too much time with that old queer, Mick." Dan winced as if the word had caused him physical pain. "Oh? Didn't you know? He used to prey on little boys like you before he came here. Just another one of our monstrous residents."

Jenny stepped forward, bringing her face close to Anna's. The other woman looked surprised and wary.

"You use that word a lot," Jenny said in a low voice. "Learned it looking in the mirror, did you?"

The slap came out of nowhere and sent Jenny reeling back, clutching her cheek. Then hot rage filled her and she tensed, ready to spring forward.

"Jenny, don't." Dan's voice was soft, but held a note that forced its way through her fury into her brain. The redness bled away and the world returned to a soothing green again. She forced herself to straighten, to breathe calmly.

"You're right. I'm better than her."

Anna turned to Dan. "I merely came to tell you that the backup generator has a red light on it, and Thomas suggested you take a look." She gave a smile that was filled with false sweetness. "When you've finished telling tales about your betters, of course."

Without waiting for a response, Anna turned on her heel and strode away. Jenny waited until the woman's footsteps had faded completely before she turned to Dan. She was surprised to see him staring at her, open-mouthed.

"Wow. I don't think I've seen anyone stand up to Anna that way."

Jenny rubbed her cheek and shrugged nonchalantly; the vestige of hot anger inside her turned to a glow of pride. "I just called her on her bullshit. She's a nasty piece of work. Never thought I'd say this, but maybe I can understand why Thomas looks around for other women.

"Anyway, thanks for showing me around. I've gotta go." She hesitated a moment, then stepped forward and hugged him. She felt him stiffen, then briefly hug her back before they parted. "Despite our eavesdropper, it really was good to see a better side of Haven." Dan's cheeks coloured but he smiled.

Jenny returned to the ladder and climbed swiftly out of the greenhouse. The cold air on her heated cheeks was welcome as she emerged into the twilight. Glancing around her to check that nothing and no one was lurking in the shadows, she headed home.

After Jenny left, Dan took some moments to sit and calm his racing heart. But every time he came close, Anna's narrowed eyes and her twisted smile as she said the word 'queer' came back into his mind.

God, if they ever find out... It was sickening to realise that sinister creatures out in the dark forest suddenly seemed less of a threat than a bitter old woman.

Eventually he found the strength to resume his watering, and the methodical, familiar task made him relax. Outside, twilight was turning to darkness. Dan switched on the strip lights they'd placed around the edges of the pool. The hanging baskets obscured a lot of their glare, but the illumination was enough to help him find his way.

Dan was refilling the watering can from one of the water butts when a noise from above made him pause. It sounded as if someone was climbing over the roof. He frowned.

That's not a person, that's an animal. Those are claws tapping on the plastic. The thought set a prickle between his shoulder blades.

The noise stopped and started, as if whatever was clambering around was moving in short bursts. And it was heading in his direction. Dan peered up and saw a shape pressed against the plastic. A strange pressure was building within his chest and it was getting difficult to breathe — almost as if the air was trying to push him back.

Dan could make out the impression of what seemed to be human hands and bare feet. The grubby plastic made it difficult to see much beyond that except a silhouette.

"Hey!" His voice wobbled slightly. "Who's there?"

The figure tensed. Silence pressed close around Dan, as if it was a physical thing. There was the grating sound of nails on plastic, as the thing above flexed its fingers. The lights around the greenhouse started to flicker.

Don't go out. Please don't go out.

Dan's heart was hammering, his ears buzzing in the silence, and although his legs tensed, ready to run, he couldn't will himself to move.

The figure brought its head low, gazing down through the roof. Dan could see an oval face with two eyes and a mouth, but there the similarities to a human stopped. There was either no nose or a nose so squashed as to be unrecognisable. The skin was incredibly pale and there was a redness around its puckered mouth. Matted hair fell to its shoulders. Its eyes seemed completely black.

The creature's thin lips pulled back into a hiss that was audible even through the plastic. Then pain erupted in Dan's head, as a hanging basket collided with his temple. He stumbled backwards, holding his head and seeing stars. When his vision came back to normal, he saw that only one hanging basket was swinging wildly; the rest remained perfectly motionless.

As if someone pushed it. He looked around, but he was alone in the greenhouse.

Dan grasped the basket and stilled it. He looked up but the figure had vanished. Outside was only the blackness of night.

Shaken to his core, Dan rubbed his chest, grateful that the unpleasant pressure had vanished. He looked around the greenhouse once again. The lights were back on, but that did little to dispel the terror that had rooted itself inside him.

CHAPTER NINE

One night, a week after being shown round the greenhouse, Jenny was walking to Mick's house and reflecting on her time in Haven. She was annoyed to discover that she was beginning to feel at home. Despite her distaste for the place, she'd fallen into a familiar routine. Most of her days were spent with the animals, which she enjoyed, apart from the bees. She sweated in the thick white suit every time she had to collect honey and the constant drone of the bees made her head ache.

She was learning her tasks as quickly as possible in the hope that Samuel would stop hovering around her when she was more competent. She would turn round and find him standing a few paces behind, just watching her. He always had a perfectly plausible reason for being there, but she hated the thought that he'd been staring at her without her noticing.

She'd also started to consider her new acquaintances as actual friends. The two old dears, Millicent and Esme, were so eccentric and generous that Jenny quickly became fond of them. Whenever she passed their door, they'd invite her into their lodge, which was decked floor to ceiling with chintzy bric-a-brac. She would come away with her face aching from smiling so much, and with her stomach full from the biscuits they were always cooking.

There was also Mick, who made her laugh whenever they spoke. And there was Dan. He was shy and awkward around her at times, but when he relaxed, he was funny and kind and full of enthusiasm for his plants. She was growing really fond of him.

Jenny had soon learned that Mick was the font of all knowledge when it came to Haven. She'd been trying to think up a way to approach him and ask him what had been going on. There was a definite edge to the commune, that she felt sure had something to do with the strange things she'd experienced herself. In the end, she'd asked Mick if she could walk Apollo with him on one of his night rounds. He'd looked at her with surprise, but agreed. "Would do him good to have some new people bossing him around, I guess."

That evening, she had told Pamela her plans, sensing that lying would only backfire on her. Her mother positively enthused over the idea.

"How wonderful of him! It really does look like you're settling in well, Jenny. I'm so pleased."

You wouldn't be so pleased if you knew I was trying to dig up dirt on this place so we can leave.

As she approached the main gates that night, Jenny saw that Mick and Apollo were already waiting. The old man wore a tattered but thick duffel coat. Mick pointed down a side path towards the chickens and goats. "This way first. You got a torch?" Jenny nodded and they set off.

Mick took them patrolling along paths that Jenny would never had known existed if they hadn't been pointed out to her. Some were no more than game trails.

"And you do this every night?" she asked, as she pushed her way past an overgrown holly tree.

"Yup. Every night. I like it. Just me and Apollo out here, you know? None of the politics you get round the dinner table. The Code doesn't matter when it's just you and the darkness."

Jenny looked at her surroundings. Even if she shone her torch straight into the forest, the range wasn't that far, and she was acutely conscious of the impenetrable blackness beyond. She tried to dispel the growing unease from her mind, to concentrate on Mick's calming presence and his entertaining chatter.

They headed towards the fields to check on the horses and then down a side path to check on the equipment shed that housed the farm machinery. Then they made their way back to the lodges, before ending up beyond the car park.

"Let's stop for a bit, shall we?" Mick said, leaning against a tree. Apollo sat at his feet without command. "My old bones can't tolerate this night air for too long." He reached inside his coat to pull out a lighter and a packet of cigarettes. He gave her a sidelong look. "I'd offer you one but they're dirty, filthy things. You keep your lungs clean and pretty."

"Are lungs pretty?" she asked with amusement.

"I can't imagine there isn't anything about you that isn't pretty, girl," he said with a wink.

Jenny laughed. Unlike Samuel's unwelcome touches or Thomas's lecherous glances, Mick's smutty comments didn't bother her at all. She felt safe with him.

"Ah, here comes the third member of our party." Mick nodded back down the path. Jenny turned and saw Dan walking towards them. When he saw Jenny, surprise registered on his face. He approached cautiously.

"What's going on?"

Jenny scowled at Mick. "Yeah, I'd like to know too. This feels like some kind of setup to me."

Mick chuckled. "Playing at matchmaking was never my thing, even in my younger days. Besides, something tells me you two aren't suited to each other." Jenny didn't fail to catch the brief but meaningful look Mick threw at Dan, and comprehension dawned. Then she felt a stab of pity as she recalled Anna's harsh words. *Poor boy. It's not going to be easy for him here when everyone finds out.*

"So why are we here?" Dan asked, digging his hands deep into his pockets.

Mick blew out a smoke ring. "An exchange of information. It strikes me that we all know a little bit, and if we pool our knowledge, we might get a step closer to figuring out what's going on here. Agreed?" They both nodded. "Good. To show willing, I'll go first."

Jenny listened as Mick described all he had seen and heard. When he described the strange face Millicent had seen at her window, Jenny thought back to her first night when she too had seen a frightening face in the undergrowth outside. Mick went on to say how several people had come up to him at breakfast at different times and commented that they thought they'd heard a deer or a large dog running through the woods the night before. Jenny glanced at the trees around her and pulled her coat tighter.

Then Dan took over. He talked about the noises he'd heard with Mick. When he'd told them about the creature crawling over the greenhouse, Jenny asked, "What do you think it was?"

He looked uncomfortable. "I didn't get a good look at it but... You know how sometimes you just feel things? Like deep down?"

"Primal instinct," Mick muttered.

"Exactly. I had this gut feeling that what was up there was human but also... not really."

Jenny thought of the car park, that silhouette rising up from the darkness and the pressure on her chest, forcing her back. She listened to the creak of trees and the whispering of the wind. Right now, the idea of something unnatural running free in the woods didn't seem so farfetched.

"Your turn, lass," Mick said.

Jenny described in as much detail as she could the face she'd seen in the bushes and her experience in the car park. When she'd finished, Dan turned to Mick and asked, "Do you think it could be linked to the witch?"

Mick snorted. "That's just a story, lad."

"Not one I've heard," Jenny said eagerly. "What witch?"

"There was no witch," Mick grumbled, "just a daft, love-sick woman who chose the wrong man to fall for."

"I think we should tell her," Dan said in a quiet voice. Mick glared at him. Jenny watched the two of them face off and was surprised when Mick crumbled first.

"Fine." He turned to Jenny. "I'll tell you the *true* story, so you don't get idiots like this," he nodded at Dan, "filling your head with rot." He cleared his throat in the manner of a great storyteller beginning an epic. "I joined Haven not long after it was set up, but Thomas, Anna and some others were here before me. Marguerite Laurent was one of them. She was quite young and pretty. She'd been a French exchange student once, and had come back over here to stay. I'm not sure of her history, but I think she worked with Thomas at the university, or had been one of his students, or something. No one really talked about it, but it was clear there was a history there. Her and Anna did not see eye to eye.

"We muddled along for a few months. Esme and Millicent joined, and then Samuel turned up. That was what you call, oh, what's the word?"

He took a long drag on his cigarette, his eyebrows drawing together as he thought hard. "The catalyst! That's it.

"When he appeared, everything started going wrong. He insisted that we draw up this Code and, because he's a relative of the original founders, people agreed. I think most of us wondered what harm it could do.

"As it turned out, quite a lot."

Mick took another drag, the light from the cigarette illuminating his features before they were reclaimed by shadows again. He blew the smoke out in a slow, steady stream.

"You see, we already had an informal code -- things like shutting the animals in and having a signing in book for the fire regs, but Anna and Samuel added other things, such as a ban on extra-marital affairs. They said it was to preserve harmony within Haven, and none of us could really go against such logic. But everyone knew Thomas and Marguerite were at it behind Anna's back. You could tell from the way the woman looked at Thomas, wide-eyed, lips slightly parted, as if just waiting for him to kiss her. So Anna used this Code as a way to get rid of Marguerite. She and Samuel bullied the poor woman and also put pressure on Thomas. In the end, Thomas cared more for his reputation than he did for Marguerite. He'd become a sort of leader for us all and wasn't about to give that up for a floozy. So he claimed that she was harassing him and insisted that she leave.

"That fair broke poor Marguerite. At first she begged and pleaded. I remember her on her knees, weeping and clutching at Thomas's jacket. But he refused to bend. In the end, they emptied her house, dumping all her possessions on the ground. That's when things turned nasty. Marguerite must've realised that things were over. She turned real vicious. She threw herself at Thomas, clawing at his face and trying to bite him. She was like a wild animal. In the end, we had to drag her off him.

"Even then, with one of us holding each arm, she wriggled and squirmed, shouting threats at Thomas and all of us. Then all of a sudden, she went still. It was disturbing, creepy, you know? She went from this frenzied madwoman to quiet, cold and cruel. She said a load of strange, unpleasant things; she claimed she was a witch and would curse us all. She told us how depraved Thomas's appetites were. She was smiling such a sweet smile when she asked Anna, "And just how will you cope with indulging them once I'm gone?"

"At that, Thomas slapped her so hard that she tumbled to the ground. He called her a liar and a whore. Then he and Samuel physically dragged her to the gates, locking her out and got the rest of us to haul her stuff to the fence and throw it over."

When Mick stopped talking, silence flowed around them. Even the forest was quiet. Jenny swallowed then said quietly, "That's horrible."

"Yeah. Weren't a nice sight to see."

"What happened to her?"

"Well, Thomas and Samuel and Anna all said she crawled back to wherever she'd come from with her tail between her legs. But a couple of people, most of whom aren't here anymore, said that they glimpsed her in the forest. You see, there are other buildings on this land. We just inhabit this lot because it's the most convenient, what with them being close to the main hut and connected to sewers. They said she'd holed up in one of the unfinished lodges in the woods. Thomas dismissed those rumours at first, saying they were imagining things. But the rumours didn't go away. People started believing she really was a witch, and she was living in the forest. It made people jittery and Thomas was forced to take action. He and Samuel went out into the forest one night. The rest of us waited in the main hut, sitting in the heaviest silence I've ever experienced. Samuel and Thomas came back in the early hours. Said they'd found a tramp, but had escorted them to the edge of the forest and called the police."

"Did you believe them?" Jenny asked.

Mick took his time replying. "I don't know. Those days are all muddled in my memory." He took a final drag on his cigarette, his eyes appearing dark and depthless in the glow. He threw it to the floor and crushed it under his boot. "But I do remember seeing that they had scratches on their hands and dirt under their fingernails, like they'd been digging. And the only time I ever need to dig in this forest, is when I have to bury something."

CHAPTER TEN

The next afternoon, Jenny slipped away from lunch early. Dan was waiting for her behind Elm Lodge, as she'd told him to. "I didn't see you in the main hut," she said as she approached. "Did you get anything to eat?"

Dan shook his head. "I couldn't, not knowing what we're about to do."

Jenny marched into the forest. "It'll be fine. No one will know, not if we're quick."

Dan hurried after her. "There are loads of stories about this place. People say the house... that it pushes you away."

Jenny felt a tingle of unease, remembering the pressure she'd felt in the car park. That had felt as if she was being pushed backwards. And Dan had felt the same thing in the greenhouse, so he'd said.

"They're just stories," she said. "Mick told us as much last night."

"No, they're true. One woman had a heart attack at the witch's lodge and nearly died." His voice and his eyes lowered. "Mum would kill me if she found out I'd gone there."

"Then let's make sure she doesn't. This way?" Jenny pointed; Dan nodded.

For a while, Jenny enjoyed being in the wood. It was a beautifully warm spring day, the sun making the leaf canopy shine an emerald green. The birds were singing and the air had the delicate scent of spring flowers. The only dark cloud was Dan, walking beside her. Feeling that the tension between them was her fault, Jenny tried to start a conversation.

"You didn't leave me something on my step the other day, did you?"

"No. Like what?"

"Well, like flowers, but not flowers. Twigs and mud and stuff like that. It was a few days ago. Really weird. Mum said it was leaf litter, but it looked like it had been placed there deliberately, that's all. Like an offering. And I thought, well, you and I are the same age and all—"

"It wasn't me," he said, a little too quickly.

Jenny smiled. "No, I didn't think it was."

"Then why did you ask?"

"I wanted to be sure, before I jumped to conclusions."

Dan looked as if he was about to say something, then changed his mind.

Jenny asked tentatively, "Have you ever given a gift to a girl?"

Dan considered this. "I once gave Marcie Brown an eraser when I was in year four. It had a rainbow on it, and she loved them. But I don't think so, apart from that."

"Uh huh." She paused, then took the plunge. "Ever given any boys any gifts?"

"Yeah, loads," he said with an uneasy laugh. "Birthday presents and all that."

Jenny stopped and waited until he was looking at her. "I like you. We're friends. You can tell me anything, if you need to, if you want to talk. I won't tell anyone."

He held a gaze for a moment, before looking away and thrusting his hands into his pockets. He started walking. "This way."

When they found the lodge rumoured to be the witch's house, it was along the same design as those at Haven, but had two storeys instead of one. Its condition was appalling. The roof was practically nonexistent, the walls on one side had completely crumbled away, and the front door had rotted at the bottom.

Dan halted, his face pale. "There. You've seen it. Can we go now?"

"I'm going to look inside."

"You can't!"

Jenny gave him a grin. "Why else do you think I came out here? You don't have to. Why don't you just go home? I can find my way back."

Dan's eyes flicked from her to the dilapidated lodge and back again. "I shouldn't..." He swallowed. "Are you sure?"

"Perfectly. Go get yourself some lunch." She gave him a brief, tight hug.

"Okay, well... be careful," he warned, before heading back along the path much faster than he'd come.

Jenny did a slow circuit to see if there was an easy way into the lodge, but her best option seemed to be trying the front door. She examined it. Broken guttering above meant that it was rotten and splintering. There was a jagged hole at the bottom, just wide enough to squeeze through. Taking a deep breath, she got down on hands and knees and crawled through the gap. The floor was wet and slimy beneath her hands, leaving dark patches on her jeans. She wiped her palms on them as she stood up and looked around. The interior was dim, the sunlight struggling to penetrate grimy windows. She wrinkled her nose at the smell that pervaded the building, the same ammonia scent she'd smelt outside her window and on the offering on her step.

It's pee, she realised suddenly. *God, what kind of animal makes that stench?*

She did a cautious tour of the ground floor. The corridor led to one large L-shaped room comprising a dining-kitchen in one section and a living room in the other. It was disgustingly dirty but intact. She placed a foot on the stairs, intending to explore the first storey, which was mostly open to the elements, but the rotten wood creaked ominously beneath her foot and she decided against it.

She went back into the main room and looked around. The cooker in the kitchen was rusted, the hob covered in twigs. The door was missing off the fridge, the interior of which was filled with black mould. Dust, dirt and twigs covered the countertop. The dining table was riddled with holes from woodworm and had a large crack running down the middle. Three wooden chairs were surprisingly clean and upright, although a fourth lay in pieces.

The living room contained a dirty sofa with its springs showing and an armchair that had rags piled on it, looking like a large nest of some kind.

A fox, maybe? Or a stray dog? Or a tramp?

On the other side of the sofa she found a pile of animal bones; chicken and fish, she guessed. She saw a little mouse skull, its nose jagged and broken.

Nauseated by the sights and smell, Jenny came to the conclusion that there were no answers to be found here. She was just turning to go when a flash of sunlight on metal caught her attention. The corner of a small tin cracker box was poking from a hole in the sofa.

Jenny crouched down and immediately sprang back up, clutching at her chest. It was as if an invisible hand had squeezed her heart and an unseen mouth had sucked all the breath out of her body.

"Steady now," she murmured, getting her heartbeat and breathing back under control. She glanced down at the innocuous box.

I should leave it.

No, that's what she wants.

A breeze ruffled her hair and Jenny felt certain that someone was standing at her shoulder. She spun round. The room was empty.

"I'm going to take it," she said out loud, "whether you want me to or not."

Glaring at the empty air, she turned back round and knelt down, slowly this time. Her heart and her breath sped up, but she couldn't tell if that was a result of her own nervousness or something more sinister trying to force her back. She reached for the box and pain shot up her arm, circling round her heart again. She gritted her teeth and leaned forward. She felt as if someone beside her was pressing close, as they too leaned forward for the box. Her neck muscles tensed painfully as she fought the urge to look back. Then her fingers brushed the cold metal of the tin and she felt a jolt of electricity that made her jump. She stopped herself from snatching her hand back and instead grasped the box firmly. The cold travelled up her arm, chasing away the pain that had been there only moments before.

Jenny drew the box out and sat back against the sofa, breathing heavily. She watched the room, waiting to see if anything further happened. She listened to the birdsong outside and the wind rustling the spring leaves for some time. Then she opened the box. The hinges were rusty and the metal warped, making doing so a struggle. She stared at the contents with curiosity. There was a pearl necklace, a rusted set of keys and some pieces of paper marked with faded writing.

Jenny picked up the papers and examined them more closely. The words were just about legible; she could see they were French. She felt a coldness creeping through her and the walls seemed to press closer. She folded the papers and put them in her pocket.

A low growl sounded from the sofa at her back. She froze. The growl came again. From the corner of her eye, she saw the seat cushions dip, as something climbed onto them.

It must have been behind the sofa all this time.

Jenny's mouth was dry, her heart hammering her chest. She had nothing to defend herself with and she had a horrible feeling that whatever was behind her would definitely be stronger and faster than her.

I mustn't run. If it's a stray dog or something, I need to show it I'm more of a threat than it expects. That's the only option.

Jenny took a deep breath and leaped up. She spun round, raising the tin above her head and screaming out a wordless cry. But the creature was already flying towards her, an indistinguishable blur of matted hair, sharp talons and teeth. The creature's momentum brought it smashing into Jenny's shoulder and chest, winding her. The world spun as she fell. She caught a glimpse of human eyes set into a monstrous face, then pain blossomed along her spine and the back of her head as she hit the ground. She twisted and sat up, alert for another attack. She glimpsed the creature's foot disappearing through the door to the hallway. Then she heard the scrabble of claws on wood, before everything fell quiet.

Jenny sat up, her breath coming hard and fast. It took her quite some time to gather enough courage to stand and walk to the front door. She clutched her back, which ached dully from her fall. She started every time the house creaked or birds fluttered in the top storey.

When she reached the front door, Jenny knelt slowly and peered out.

I'm going to have to stick my head through first if I want to get out. Thoughts of the creature waiting just beyond the door, ready to rip her head off, kept her crouching there for at least ten minutes. Realising there was no other means of escape, Jenny tensed herself then shot forward, scrambling through the hole as fast as she could. Her coat got caught on a broken shard and, for a terrible moment, she thought an unseen hand was hauling her back inside. But then the fabric ripped and she tumbled forward onto the broken porch.

She paused, catching her breath and taking in her surroundings. The forest was still and empty. Jenny scrambled up and headed back towards Haven at a run, not slowing until she glimpsed the main hut through the trees. Even then, she walked at a fast pace, constantly looking over her shoulder until she was safely back inside Ash Lodge.

CHAPTER ELEVEN

Dan had felt like a shit from the moment he'd turned his back on Jenny outside the witch's lodge. He'd always been frightened by the stories of the witch, but he felt he should have overcome that fear in Jenny's company. Yet when he'd been in the wood, the thought of entering that ruined building had made his stomach flip.

He'd seen his chance to make amends when everyone was coming out of the main hut after a dinner of stew and dumplings. As Jenny had paused to pull her hood up against the rain, he walked past and whispered, "Meet me by the goats tonight at ten o'clock."

She'd glanced at him in surprise then nodded.

Dan spent the evening thinking through what he might say. At a quarter to ten that night he said to his mother, "Just popping out, Mum."

She looked up from her book, a small smile on her face. "Meeting someone?"

Dan could feel the blush creeping over his cheeks. "Just Mick."

"Oh? Not Jenny then?"

A lump rose in Dan's throat. "No."

"Okay, well, take a torch anyway," she said, going back to her book.

Dan hesitated a moment to see if she had any more to say. When she didn't, the tension between his shoulders eased and he headed out the door.

He was relieved to see the day's constant rain had ceased. The world had a damp, sharp smell to it and the road shone wetly in the moonlight. He arrived at the animal enclosures five minutes early and spent the time pacing, making a deep groove in the soft mud. He still hadn't fixed upon what to say and when Jenny finally arrived, the words tumbled out of him. "I'm sorry, Jenny, I shouldn't have left you. It was really shitty of me and I've felt bad about it all of yesterday *and* today and—"

"Hey, it's okay," she said with a smile. She reached out and rubbed his arm. Her touch was surprisingly comforting.

"So, we're still friends?" he asked hesitantly.

She grinned. "Definitely. If we weren't friends, would I show you what I found?"

Trepidation filled him. "You found something? At the witch's lodge?"

"Yes. Look." She put her hand in her pocket and pulled out some folded pieces of paper. She offered them to him. Dan was reluctant to take them, but she just kept holding them out, and eventually he gave in.

He flicked through them. The paper was old and yellowed, corners and edges crumbling a bit. His eyes scanned the words. His throat constricted. "They're in French."

"I know. I found them in a tin box inside the witch's house."

That sent a shiver down his spine. Dan's heartbeat thumped in his ears. Your mum has a languages degree, yes? Give it to her."

"No way. She'd kill me if she found out I'd been there."

"Then tell her I went on my own." She gave him a sly look. "After all, you did leave me."

Guilt set Dan's stomach churning.

"I'm not giving it to her, but I'll use her dictionaries and try to translate it, if you like?"

She looked at him with surprise. "You can speak French?"

"A bit. You don't grow up with a language teacher as a mother without learning how to ask for breakfast in three different languages."

Jenny laughed; Dan did too. It felt good. His initial apprehension was ebbing away and curiosity was taking its place. He really did want to know what was in these papers.

"Good," Jenny said. "Now let's go home. It's bloody freezing."

Dan walked Jenny back to the main road and they parted at the side road leading to Ash Lodge. She hugged him, her breath warm on his ear, before she hurried towards the clearing. Dan turned away, feeling warmth radiate through him. It had been so long since he'd had a proper friend.

He dug his hands into his coat pockets and his fingers brushed the paper. It felt greasy against his skin and he pulled his hand out quickly.

Jesus, what have I got myself into?

CHAPTER TWELVE

Jenny glanced behind her when she was halfway up the road to Ash Lodge, and saw Dan walking away.

He really does care about me. The idea gave her a warm glow inside. She'd felt so isolated and angry since Pamela had dragged her here, it was nice to have a real connection with someone.

And I need to be a better friend to him, she thought resolutely. *I shouldn't ask him such prying questions. I mustn't force him into the woods to look for cursed lodges.* Her step faltered. *And I probably shouldn't have given him those pages to translate. Damn. I've just dragged him deeper into all this. But I can't do it on my own.*

There was a rustling to her right. Jenny froze. The grass swayed then stilled.

A mouse, bound to be. Or a rat. Jenny felt her skin crawl at the thought. She continued towards Ash Lodge, her steps faster now. Their lodge was the only one with light coming from the window, and the clearing seemed particularly gloomy. Her skin prickled, as if the windows of the empty lodges were the eyes of waiting beasts.

As she climbed the steps to the porch, the front door opened and her mother stepped out, carrying a bin bag.

"Ah, Jenny," she said, smiling. She held out the bag. "You're in your outdoor clothes already – could you take this to the bins please?"

Jenny felt pressure between her shoulder blades, as if something was watching her. "Leave it for the morning, Mum."

"I can't. The bag's split and there's something leaking out of it."

"Then put it in another bin bag."

"There isn't one. Look, it's fine. I'll do it—"

"No, Mum. *I'll* do it." Jenny grabbed the bag.

"You're an angel, thank you."

Pamela shut the door and Jenny turned, digging her torch out of her pocket. She examined the bag; it was indeed leaking. As much as she didn't like the idea of going out into the night alone, she liked the thought of her mother going out even less.

Jenny strode back to the road, holding the dripping bag away from her. A light drizzle had started to fall, the raindrops sharp and cold against her skin. She lowered her head, protecting her face from the worst of it.

Halfway along the main road, she turned left, going up a little path that ran behind some of the lodges and led into the forest. The bins were set about a quarter of a mile away, so that their smell wouldn't disturb any of the residents. The path was twisty, but solar-powered lampposts lined it and provided some illumination.

Jenny shone her torch from side to side. The drizzle was a fine rain, plastering her hair to her head and getting in her eyes. She scanned the woods for movement, trying to force out of her mind the image from yesterday of that creature launching itself at her.

The large bins were stored underneath a sloping roof of corrugated iron supported by four wooden posts. Jenny stood in front of the enclosure, shining her torch into every gap to check nothing unpleasant was hiding in there.

Warily she approached the general rubbish bin. She slung her bag in, closed the lid with a clang and then looked up. The rain had grown heavier. The drops pounded on the sheet metal above her, creating a dull din.

Jenny walked to the edge of the shelter and looked out. By the illumination of the path lights, she could see about fifteen feet ahead of her, but beyond that the trees became indistinct, before merging with the darkness completely.

Beneath the drumming of the rain on the roof, Jenny heard the erratic patter of water running off leaves into puddles. Combined, the noises were strangely comforting, like the white noise of the city. The forest was normally too quiet for her liking. She breathed in deeply and then let out her breath slowly, steam curling before her face.

Something ran between the trees, at the very edge of the light. Jenny focused on the spot, scanning the trees for more movement. Out of the corner of her eye, she saw something deeper into the forest, moving away from her.

Suddenly the susurration of the rain was too loud. Jenny concentrated on listening for any noise above the sound of the water and her own heartbeat. Her eyes flicked from shadow to shadow, waiting for the fleeting shape to reappear.

A fox barked somewhere behind her, making Jenny jump. "Screw this," she muttered and stepped out of the bin store. The rain hammered painfully onto her sodden scalp, but she didn't care.

It was heading away from the lodges, into the forest. It shouldn't come after me. Yet Jenny still glanced over her shoulder every few steps, wiping the water out of her eyes as it ran in rivulets down her face. When she was finally back on the road, she pelted along the broken tarmac towards Ash Lodge, telling herself that she was only running to get out of the rain.

The sun rose the next morning in a clear blue sky, all the

rainclouds banished. A fresh, clean scent hung over the commune, but Dan couldn't find it in himself to appreciate such natural beauty. Filled with worries about what he had done, what he hadn't done, and what he had yet to do, he hadn't slept. To his weary eyes, the sun seemed too bright and the sky painful in its blueness.

At breakfast, he settled himself down at a quiet table, far away from everyone else. The freshly baked bread and hand churned butter tasted like greasy cardboard in his mouth.

To his horror, Jenny placed her bowl opposite him and sat down. "Have you started on the translation yet?" she asked in an excited whisper.

"No," Dan snapped. "You only gave it to me last night and I needed to sleep and do chores and... things."

"Oh. Of course. Sorry. I didn't mean to bug you about it." Jenny stared down at her muesli.

Dan sighed. "It's okay. I'll start it today. I promise."

Jenny grinned; Dan found a smile spreading over his own lips as well.

Breakfast in Jenny's company passed more pleasantly than he thought it would, and eased the tension that knotted his muscles. By the time he rose to take his empty plate to the serving hatch, Dan's mood was considerably lighter.

When he got home, his mother was already there, making a second cup of tea. She smirked at him and his heart lurched.

"I saw you chatting to Jenny."

"Yeah, she's a friend. Am I not allowed to have friends? I thought you were the one who wanted me to get to know her?"

Selena held up her hands in surrender. "Sorry, Dan. I didn't mean to pester you. I just want you to get to know her and have some fun." She paled and added quickly, "Just safe fun, you know, like friends..." She tailed off, looking uncomfortable.

Dan laughed and hugged her. He was surprised when she returned his embrace very tightly. He gently eased himself away and saw tears glistening on her eyelashes.

"You know, I'm your mother. I love you. You can tell me anything."

Dan stiffened, but kept his voice soft. "I know, Mum. And I will. If I have anything to tell. But I've got some stuff to do. I said I'd help Jenny out with... a project. You know, safe fun." He grinned. She laughed.

"Off you go then."

She turned away, busying herself in the kitchen. Dan took one of her dictionaries off the bookcase and then headed into his own room. He dug out a notebook, spread the papers out on his bed, and settled down with the dictionary on his knee. Looking at the pages made him feel queasy with apprehension, but he forced such feelings aside.

"Right," he murmured, "let's see what you have to say, Marguerite."

CHAPTER THIRTEEN

Jenny felt on edge with anticipation all that day and the next. She snapped at Samuel, his proximity irritating her more than usual.

She desperately wanted to learn what was written on those pages, and knew if she went anywhere near Dan, she'd only pester him about it. That wouldn't be acting like the good friend she'd promised herself she'd be. So when she and Pamela went to the main hut for their meals, Jenny steadfastly refused even to look in Dan's direction.

By eight o'clock that night, Jenny was fraught and weary. She was in bed by nine and asleep within moments.

Jenny started awake, uncertain what had roused her. Her skin was chilled and her stomach felt full and uncomfortable. Her clock said the time was almost eleven. She stared at the wall, listening to the racing of her own heart. She heard her mother's gentle snores behind her.

A foul stench assailed Jenny's nostrils and she tensed. She detected raspy breathing, low and quiet. It didn't match Pamela's snoring behind her. Jenny squeezed her eyes shut, telling herself she was imagining it. Yet the noise continued. The seconds ticked by. A wet gurgle broke the rasping rhythm and Jenny stifled a frightened groan.

She felt Pamela sit up in bed next to her. "What on earth—?" Pamela began as she switched on her bedside lamp. Jenny saw the figure crouched by their wardrobe. Its shape was mostly human, but the creature's arms were slightly too long, its face slightly too angular and lacking a fully formed nose. Patches of skin appeared grey and peeling beneath a layer of dirt and matted hair. Its lips were black with red sores around them. The dark eyes narrowed in the sudden light. The figure hissed then bolted for the door. Pamela screamed and clutched the duvet to her chest, but Jenny tumbled out of bed and rushed to the open front door. She grabbed onto the jamb to stop herself flying off the porch. She stared at the trees surrounding their lodge, lit by the porch light. The woodland was silent and still. It had swallowed without trace whatever creature had been lurking in their home.

Jenny closed the door, trying to force down the fear she felt rising within her. She returned to the bedroom to find her mother on the phone.

"Yes, we'll wait right here. I promise." Pamela put the phone down.

"Who did you call?"

"Thomas. He said we could call him any time and he'd help. He's coming over."

"Great," said Jenny sourly. "Then we'd better put some clothes on."

When Jenny was dressed, she returned to the front door and stared at the forest.

Is it still out there? What the hell was it? Was it human or animal or... something else? She shuddered.

"Everything okay?" Mick's voice from the darkness startled her. He was walking up the side road towards the lodge, Dan behind him. "I saw your lights on and your door open. Has something happened?"

"Yes. There was someone – or something – in our house just now. It was like a human, but also not. I can't explain it very well and I didn't get a good look. Mum's called Thomas and he's coming over."

"How reassuring." Mick's voice dripped with disdain.

"I don't suppose you guys could hang around too, could you?" Jenny asked hopefully.

Dan, who until then had hung back a little, stepped forward. "Of course we will." His voice was steady, but his wide eyes betrayed his fear.

Jenny smiled. "Thank you."

Dan joined Jenny on the porch and they stood silently together as Mick did a circuit of the clearing. He came back, frowning. "There's lots of patches of flattened grass as if..." he hesitated, glancing at Jenny.

"Go on," she urged.

"As if someone has been crouching there, watching the house."

Jenny felt as if her guts had vanished leaving a cold emptiness inside her. "Watching? The house?"

"Yes, but it could be anything. Might have been a badger stopping to eat a meal or a fox lying in wait for prey. Don't read too much into it."

He reached out and squeezed her shoulder, but Jenny took little comfort from the gesture.

Pamela appeared behind them. "Oh, am I glad to see you," she said to Dan and Mick. Her gaze travelled beyond them and her face lit up in a relieved smile. "And Thomas too. Thank you for coming. And... Samuel, is that you?"

Thomas strode up to the house, Samuel trailing in his wake, his eyes on the ground. "It is indeed," said Thomas, standing in front of them. "I got out as soon as I heard your call. I bumped into Samuel on the way here and he agreed to come with me. For reinforcements."

"Just bumped into him?" said Mick. There was real venom in his voice. "What were you doing out at this time, Samuel?"

"None of your concern," Samuel snapped, glaring at him.

Thomas pushed through them all to stand by Pamela and put a reassuring arm around her shoulder. "Tell me what happened."

"There was someone in our room," Pamela began, her voice shaking slightly. "It was a man I think, but he was in a costume or something, and had a mask on. He was just... staring at us. Oh, it was so horrible!" She buried her face in Thomas's shoulder and her body shook with sobs. Thomas patted her back and shushed her gently.

Disgusted, Jenny stepped away from them. The movement drew Thomas's gaze and he glared at her. But as Pamela pulled away, his expression immediately softened and he said gently, "We've been having some trouble with some teenage kids recently, and it sounds like they've taken it a step further by breaking into your home. We'll go out into the forest and find them. Won't we?" he added, looking meaningfully at the other men.

Jenny stepped forward, meeting his gaze with a steely stare. "Yes, we will."

Thomas shook his head. "You stay here with your mother and—"

"I'm going," Jenny said firmly. Thomas's gaze hardened.

To Jenny's surprise, Dan stepped forward, standing shoulder-to-shoulder with her. "I think Jenny can look after herself, plus she's the only one of us that's actually seen this thing, so I think it's a good idea to take her with us."

Thomas glared at them both and was drawing breath to reply when Mick said, quietly but firmly, "I agree."

Thomas tilted his head back, looking down his nose at

them. "Fine. An extra pair of eyes will be useful." He turned to Pamela with a smile that sickened Jenny. His voice was like honey. "You go inside, Pamela, and shut the door. Stay safe."

"But Jenny—"

"I'll be fine, Mum," Jenny said, buttoning up her coat. "Besides, I've got four men here to protect me," she added, knowing that this line of reasoning above all else was likely to appeal to her mother.

Pamela bit her lip but nodded. "Very well. Just stay close to them, and do as they say, okay?"

Jenny gave a tight smile, which seemed to satisfy Pamela who went inside and closed the door.

Thomas rubbed his hands together. "Right then. Let's go hunting." He turned and strode down the steps. As he passed Samuel, Jenny heard him whisper, "Your flies are undone."

CHAPTER FOURTEEN

The sky was cloudless, the air cold. A bright full moon shone above them as they walked across the clearing. Mick showed them where the patches of flattened grass were, as well as a broken tree branch directly opposite Ash Lodge.

"Whoever it was, they went this way," he said.

Thomas nodded and walked into the forest. Jenny followed with the others, her boots squelching in the mud. Everyone had torches, so the trees were illuminated for a good twenty feet in every direction. Yet somehow that made Jenny feel even more vulnerable; the brightness only emphasised the dark forest beyond the reach of their torchlight. She felt as if they were in a bubble, with darkness and wilderness pressing at the edge.

"You'll never find anything like this," Mick grumbled.

"Like what?" Thomas snapped.

"Lit up, making a cacophony. We need to be quiet, like. As silent as possible. Just one torch."

"Then it'll be mine staying on," said Thomas imperiously.

Everyone else switched their torch off. Thomas, Samuel and Daniel picked up large sticks as weapons. They spread out in a line through the forest, each silent and looking around them. Jenny was near one end of the line, with Mick at the far end on her right.

Standing still brought a chill to her bones. She wrapped her arms around her, trying to trap the warmth. She shuffled her feet, flexing her toes to stop them from going numb. She let her arms drop to her side and felt

Mick's fingers entwine with hers. She was grateful for the contact.

She turned to smile at him — but Mick wasn't looking at her. He wasn't anywhere near her. He was several paces away, staring back the way they'd come.

Her gaze travelled downwards. The fingers enclosing hers were gnarled, the skin rough. An arm was extending out from a fern behind her. She twisted and saw a face between the fronds. The eyes were wide, watching her. The nose was a mangled lump; just below, a pair of thin black lips parted in a grin that revealed sharp, jagged teeth.

Jenny drew breath to scream but the fingers tightened, then tugged her backwards. Her cry was muffled by dirt and foliage as she was dragged across the forest floor. Brambles raked her face and her back struck painfully against tree roots.

She heard her companions shout, although she couldn't make out the words. Then legs were charging past her as the others caught up. The fingers around her wrist vanished, just as she heard a squeal of pain. Then Mick was helping her up.

Everyone had turned their torches back on and were pointing them at the creature, which lay curled on the ground. Blood shone wetly on its dirty skin. She recognised the rasping breath, only now the sound had an unpleasant, wet gurgle to it. The monster tried to drag itself away but its arm and one leg had been broken and it could only manage a slow, pathetic wriggle.

Jenny's horror drained away, to be replaced with pity. "What is it?"

"It looks like a man," Mick said wonderingly. "Look — it's even got a dick."

Jenny's eyes flicked downwards before she could stop

herself; she glimpsed something limp and dirty in a nest of hair, before she looked away.

"It's not human," Samuel said, his voice hard and cold. "Look at its skin. Look at its eyes. It's some hellish abomination. It needs to die."

"Wait," said Dan urgently, stepping forward and holding out a hand. "It looks like a man, we can all see that."

Samuel sneered. "Having a dick doesn't qualify you as a human. It's either an animal that needs to be disposed of, or its some kind of corrupted human..." he fixed Dan with a cold stare, "in which case it still needs to be disposed of."

"Thomas," Mick said, "what are we going to do with it?"

As if understanding, the creature lifted a hand towards Thomas. It made a whimpering noise that almost sounded like the word, "pair".

Jenny glanced at Thomas and saw something that looked like shock flash across his face; then he adopted a mask of contempt.

"Samuel's right. It's not worthy to live. It needs to die."

"Wait—" Mick said, holding out a hand, but he was too late. Thomas stepped forward and raised his hefty stick. He brought it down hard and fast, denting the creature's skull with a sickening thump. Blood splattered across his trousers. Jenny reeled back, turning away as Thomas brought the stick down two more times.

The silence that followed hummed in her ears. Jenny felt something constricting her throat, but she couldn't tell if it was manic laughter or the need to vomit. She was aware of the men talking behind her, but their words sounded muffled and distant. She turned back to stare at the mangled body. Sickness crept through her and she wished fervently that she'd never got out of bed.

For a few minutes, she zoned out, hearing nothing but her frantic heartbeat which was loud in her ears. Then a hand gripped her shoulder and she looked up into Dan's face.

"We're going to bury it," he said. His mouth twisted slightly with disgust as he spoke, but there was determination in his eyes.

Jenny nodded and they joined Mick who stood at the creature's head. Mick slid his arms under the creature's shoulders, while Jenny and Dan took a leg each. Jenny held back a grimace at the feel of the rough, hairy skin. The ammonia stink of it was almost overwhelming and Jenny only took shallow breaths to avoid breathing it in.

"What are you doing?" Thomas snapped.

"Giving it a decent burial," Mick said as they started carrying the corpse away.

"Just cover it up with twigs and dirt," Thomas told him. "The animals will soon get rid of it for us."

"It looks like a man, so it'll be buried like a man."

"It's an abomination," Samuel cut in, "but I guess you'd recognise one of your own, Mick."

Jenny glanced at Mick. The old man had pressed his lips into a thin white line, but he didn't stop moving.

"Don't expect us to help you," Thomas called out.

"I wasn't," Mick muttered.

They carried the body for about five minutes before Mick chose a suitable spot and put the body down gently.

"You wait here," he told them. "I'll get some shovels."

Jenny's legs ached and she sank gratefully to the ground as Mick walked away. Dan joined her, his movements stiff and awkward.

Neither of them spoke. Jenny listened to the distant drip of water in the forest. An owl hooted and its mate replied.

Dan glanced round at the body and then said, "I guess that's it now. No more scares."

"I hope so."

There was a pause then Dan said, "I've started on the translation."

Despite her exhaustion, Jenny's interest was piqued. "Oh yes?"

"Yeah. There's nothing very helpful in there. No names, no dates."

"But do you think Marguerite wrote it?"

He considered this. "Yes, I think so. The writer talks about being kicked out, about still being in love with "him", and I think we can guess who that is."

Jenny shook her head. "What is it about that man? Women seem to fall over themselves to be with him, but I just don't get what they see in him."

Dan shrugged. "Beats me.

"I also found out that Marguerite was pregnant like she said. She writes about the child growing in her belly."

Jenny shook her head. "Poor woman. Imagine having your baby alone in the forest." Her guts gave a sickening twist as a thought occurred to her. She slowly turned and looked at the corpse. "You don't think... *that* was her child, do you?"

Dan looked back and paled. "I... I don't know. I mean, it's hard to tell age. It might be. I don't know when Marguerite was here and whether the dates add up. I'll have to ask Mick."

"But not tonight."

"No. Not tonight."

A silence fell between them, but it was charged with tension. Jenny stared at the trees around them.

The woods are empty now. We've caught the monster. There's nothing to be afraid of out here anymore.

Deep down, she didn't feel that was true at all.

CHAPTER FIFTEEN

Over the next few days, nothing happened beyond the bluebells coming out to fill the forest with colour and a beautiful scent. Dan went about his duties in a daze. He ate with the others in the main hut as normal, but only gave monosyllabic answers to any questions put to him.

With bitterness, he saw that Thomas was his usual confident self.

I guess he feels no remorse about what he did to his own child. As soon as the thought had passed through his mind, Daniel felt bad. *Thomas didn't know it was his child. Still...*

Jenny kept her distance and he was grateful for that. He thought she'd be bugging him to keep on at the translation. But he just couldn't face it. Every time he stared down at those yellowing sheets of paper, the memory of that broken corpse came into his mind.

That night, Dan was jolted awake by a distraught scream piercing the night. He sat bolt upright in bed, his heart hammering. He listened, not only for the scream to come again, but also for the footsteps of his mother, coming to check what the noise was. But their lodge was quiet and the scream was not repeated. Dan forced his rigid body to relax.

It was just a fox or something.

Or something.

He glanced over at the table in his room, where the papers were stacked underneath the dictionary. For a moment, he had the urge to get up and see what else

Marguerite had to say.

He rolled over and closed his eyes, but sleep was a long time coming.

The next morning was crisp but cold again, as if the clement weather of the past few days hadn't happened. Dan staggered out of the door, pulling a jumper over his head. He'd slept late and only his mother knocking on his door on her way to breakfast had woken him.

He hurried up the road, squinting in the early morning sun. When he got to the main hut, it was practically deserted. He grabbed some toast and marmalade, then sat down by his mother. "Have you seen Jenny this morning?"

"Yes. She left about fifteen minutes ago. I think I overheard her say she was off with David to sell some produce at Alnwick farmer's market."

"Oh. Okay." Despondency settled over Dan. He'd wanted to ask Jenny if she'd heard the cry last night, and what she'd made of it. Now, he was filled with a restless energy. He didn't notice Thomas coming towards their table until the man was towering over them.

"Ah. Dan. Mick told me that he noticed the security light by the barn wasn't working last night. It needs to be fixed. We can't risk someone breaking in and vandalising our machinery now, can we?"

"Why? They never have before." His anxiety and tiredness gave a sharp edge to his voice.

Thomas's eyes narrowed. "I'm not sure I care for your tone, young man. That's not the way for a boy to speak to his betters."

Betters. The words lit a fire inside Dan. He stood up, stepping close to Thomas. Dan hadn't realised before but, standing up straight, he was just as tall as the older man.

Thomas's eyes widened. He took a step back.

You killed your own child. How does that make you my better?

Dan took a deep steadying breath. "I'm not a boy and you are not my better," he said firmly. Then he sat down, turning his attention back to his toast. "I'll look at the light today. When I have a moment."

The back of his neck burned and he felt sure that Thomas was staring at him. But the other man said nothing; he just walked away. Dan let out a shaky breath.

His mother leaned across the table. "Good for you," she whispered, before she taking her dirty cutlery to the hatch.

Dan finished his breakfast quickly, his head down. His anger was already cooling, and now guilt was creeping in. He shouldn't have spoken to Thomas that way. The man knew nothing about Marguerite's child. And that creature in the forest might not have been hers, even if it did seem the most plausible explanation.

After breakfast, Dan set off towards the barn. When the sun shone, it was warm on his face, but when clouds drifted across it, the world turned cold again.

The security light's problem turned out to be a faulty wire. Dan went back through the wood to his tool shed to get a screwdriver, some wire clippers and a spare bulb. He returned to find Andrea at the barn, walking out of it with the chainsaw.

She smiled at him. "Hello. Fixing the light are you?"

"Yeah."

"Thought so. I overheard your conversation with Thomas and the way you stood up to him." She gave him a conspiratorial smile. "It was good to see. You can't take too much shit off him or Anna, or else they'll walk all over you." Her look turned to one of concern. "You've not seemed yourself recently, Dan. You know you can talk to me, about anything, don't you?"

People seem to be saying that to me a lot.

But I guess I've got plenty of secrets these days.

He forced himself to smile. "Thanks. I'll remember that." He gestured to the chainsaw. "Doing some coppicing?"

"Yep. If I can remember how to work the bloody thing."

"You need to twist the dial and hold it for a few seconds to let the motor catch."

"Thanks."

Dan went to fix the light while Andrea retrieved the rest of the coppicing gear. Dan finished first and he called out a goodbye as he headed back towards Haven.

The sky was filled with grey clouds now and the wind seemed to have more bite in it. Dan kept his eyes on the path, his mind full of the day's chores to be done. He was some way from the barn when a movement made him look up.

A terrifyingly familiar creature had just stepped onto the path. Matted hair covered its grey-skinned body. Its eyes were dark, no definition between the iris and the pupil.

Oh god. We killed you. We killed you!

But then Dan saw that this wasn't the same creature. The shoulders were narrower, its body more lithe. The hair on its head was thicker, growing down to cling to its chest in a matted lump.

The creature sniffed. Its eyes narrowed and its stance changed from cautious to aggressive. Its filthy hands dug into the ground as it snarled, showing yellow teeth.

Dan could sense the creature was about to charge at

him. On instinct, he drew his hand back and threw the screwdriver. The creature dodged and hissed. Then it crouched low, tensed to spring.

The loud roar of an engine filled the woods. It took Dan a moment to realise that he was hearing the chainsaw back at the barn. The creature cowered, looking around as if it couldn't make sense of where the noise was coming from.

Dan saw his chance. He seized a large branch lying at the roots of a tree. Letting instinct overrule his fear, he charged at the confused creature.

It hissed at him, uncertain but holding its ground. Dan thought he might end up running into the monster, but almost at the last moment, the creature turned and fled into the trees.

Dan didn't stop, and he didn't drop the branch. He ran back towards Haven, catching sight of flickers of movement in the forest.

It's keeping pace with me, he realised grimly. He tightened his grip on the branch.

Dan headed straight to Holly Lodge. He stumbled through the door, dropped the branch inside then headed straight to his room. He closed the curtains and slumped down on the bed, panting heavily.

But we killed it, didn't we? What the hell?

No. It wasn't the same creature.

But it must have been. How many are there?

His gaze flicked to the desk, the pile of papers and the dictionary. He glanced at the window, wondering if the monster was still out there, biding its time.

He went to the table and pulled the pile over to him, his hands shaking. Then he started on the rest of the translation.

CHAPTER SIXTEEN

It had been a long day, but Jenny had felt elated after her trip to Alnwick. She hadn't realised just how isolated she'd felt in Haven. It was like the forest cut them off completely from the outside world. Being in the market town had revitalised her spirit.

As David had driven them home in the Land Rover, he'd chatted jovially all the way, but Jenny's mood had got darker the closer they came to Haven. As they turned off the main road and the trees closed around the car, Jenny felt a sense of claustrophobia.

She tried to battle it and find a warm smile for David as they parted company at the main hut. As she was walking back towards Ash Lodge, she saw Mick coming towards her. Even in the growing evening gloom, she could see his dark expression and it sapped away the final scraps of her good mood.

"Apollo's gone," he said, his voice raw with emotion.

"Run away?"

Mick shook his head. "Taken. I'm sure of it. The gate was open and, clever mutt though he is, he can't open gates."

Jenny glanced around, checking there was no one close by. "Do you think it might have been someone here?"

Mick chewed his bottom lip. "Maybe. Thomas has no love for me, nor Anna or Samuel, but my bones tell me this is something else. Apollo's rope was chewed through. Either he did that wild with fear or," he looked at her fearfully, "something else did."

Jenny gave a nervous laugh and reached out to rub his arm in what she hoped was a reassuring manner. "I'm sure it's nothing sinister. I'm sure there's a rational explanation."

Mick looked unconvinced. "I need you to help me look. I'd ask Dan but I haven't seen him all day and no one's answering at Holly Lodge."

"Sure. Not a problem."

They walked to Mick's place where they picked up a couple of torches. Jenny's stomach growled, telling her it was almost dinner time, but she ignored it. Mick wouldn't eat given the state he was in, and she couldn't bring herself to leave him.

"You stick close now," Mick said in a low voice as they started out into the forest. "When I was looking earlier, I swear something was following me. I could hear it sniffing."

Jenny shuddered. Suddenly the crunch of their footsteps on the forest's leaf-litter seemed uncomfortably loud. "I could have imagined it, I guess," Mick added, "but these woods just don't feel right."

"Well, now there's two of us." Jenny had meant it in a reassuring manner, but she could sense what the old man meant: walking beneath the trees felt different, more threatening, and the intensity of the feeling made her certain she wasn't imagining it.

They wandered around, calling Apollo's name. Jenny had the impression Mick was walking with some destination in mind and it soon became clear that they were heading for the creature's grave. Jenny's apprehension grew with each step. When they reached the spot, horror rolled through her in waves. Soil was scattered everywhere, exposing an empty hole.

"It... dug its way out?" she asked, her mouth dry.

Mick knelt down. "No. Look at these grooves going down. The creature was dug up."

Jenny shone her torch around, turning a full circle, examining every inch of forest. Night seemed to be gathering around them far too quickly.

An animal howl rang out, travelling straight down Jenny's spine.

"Apollo!" Mick sprinted away. Jenny followed close behind as another howl echoed through the woods.

"There!" Mick cried, shining his torch ahead. Apollo was lying on the ground, one of his front legs clearly broken, and his back legs were bound to a stake driven into the ground. Mick rushed forward.

"Wait!" Jenny called out.

A dark shape hurtled out from among the trees and slammed into Mick. The older man's torch skittered away. The creature clambered on top of the fallen man, its arms a frenzied blur of movement. Mick cried out in pain as claws slashed at his chest.

The torch Jenny held was the only weapon to hand. She rushed forward, raised the torch above her head, then brought it down hard and fast. The torch connected with the creature's head with a loud thud. The monster gave a yelp of pain and scrambled off Mick. It lashed out at Jenny, knocking the torch out of her hand.

As the torch went spinning, everything in front of Jenny became a confusion of shadows. But she could hear the creature coming for her. She raised her hands just as the monster crashed into her chest. She staggered and fell to her knees as claws savaged her hands and arms, trying to reach her face. Hot pain bloomed across her palms.

Gritting her teeth, Jenny pushed her arms out hard and fast, forcing the creature away from her. It was only a moment's respite but it was all she needed. As the creature launched itself at her again, she drew her arm back and brought her fist round in a punch that caught the creature's cheek. Blood splattered her face, warm against her chilled skin. The creature emitted a gurgling cough as it fell back. Then it turned and disappeared among the trees.

Jenny grabbed her torch, shining it in all directions. The forest was still; the creature was gone. Jenny hurried over to Mick. His wound was deep and bleeding heavily.

"We need to get you home, get that patched up."

Moving the torch to her other hand, Jenny hauled Mick to his feet. The old man groaned and slumped against her shoulder.

"Apollo," he croaked.

Jenny glanced over her shoulder. The dog was struggling to rise. She bit her lip. She wanted to get the hell out of there, but the thought of leaving Apollo behind cast a dark shadow over her heart.

"Hang on." Jenny leaned Mick against a tree. She untied Apollo's bonds. The dog got unsteadily to its feet, whining with pain.

Jenny and Mick slowly but steadily stumbled towards Mick's house, Apollo limping behind them.

As Jenny laid Mick on the sofa, the old man said in a rasping voice, "It had tits."

"What?" she replied distractedly, already on her way to the kitchen.

When she came back with the first aid kit and a bowl of freshly boiled water, he said, "That creature. It was a girl. There must have been two of them."

The horror of the idea made Jenny go numb, but she

tried to concentrate on tending Mick's wound. The old man tensed as she wiped clean his skin, the pain keeping him from speaking further. Just as she was tugging open a sterile dressing, she heard the front door open.

Dan came in, his face white. He held up the papers he was gripping.

"That thing in the woods. It's got a sister and—-" He stopped abruptly, taking in the scene before him. "What happened?"

"The sister," Jenny said grimly. "Now, help me."

While Dan supported Mick's shoulders, Jenny wrapped the dressing around him as tightly as she dared. When she was done, Dan eased Mick backwards. The old man winced with pain but when he looked at them both, his eyes were bright and alert.

"I heard that thing sniffing. I reckon it — she — hunts by scent. If she dug up her brother, then your scent and mine, as well as Samuel and Thomas's will be all over him." His eyes flicked to Dan. "You said "sister". How do you know that?"

"Jenny found some pages in the witch's lodge. They were in French. She gave them to me to translate. They were written by Marguerite. They start off with her talking about being kicked out. They're bitter but full of hope that "he" will come for her. And she's full of excitement about the baby she's carrying. But as the papers go on they get more," he licked his lips, "vicious. She stops hoping for him to come and starts hating him instead.

"When the baby is born, it's not one but two. A boy and girl. She wrote about them fondly, but even she could see they were deformed." He lifted the pages and read out, "Those that are left are idiots, all of them. They wouldn't understand us. My children aren't savages, I know it. I've torn up my pictures of him. He's never coming. I have so little time left, but I have cast charms around our home to protect my babies after I've gone. The world will not understand. They'll call them demons, but they're just children. I will not let any harm come to them, even if death separates us."

Jenny felt coldness creep through her along with the dreadful realisation. "Not only are they Marguerite's children, but she's still protecting them. That pressure I felt on my chest at the car park — it felt like I was being pushed away. It must have been one of her charms." She turned to Dan. "When you were in the greenhouse, you said you felt the same, and then a hanging basket hit you, as if it had been pushed. It's all Marguerite, trying to keep us away from them."

"Well, she's not doing a very good job at keeping them away from us," Mick muttered.

"Maybe the charms were never supposed to work that way round," Dan said. "Maybe she cast charms to keep us away from them but now her children have started exploring closer to Haven, we're experiencing the spells whenever they come near us.

"We have to warn the others," Dan said with determination. "If Mick's right and she's got our scents, she might be coming after us one at a time."

Jenny snorted. "I'm not going out there with that thing on the loose."

Dan looked at her with surprise. "But she could kill Samuel and Thomas. I know they're both fucking arseholes, but they don't deserve to die."

Taken aback by his crass language, Jenny exchanged a look with Mick who appeared equally as shocked.

"Found yourself some balls then," he commented.

Dan gave a humourless smile. "Eventually."

Jenny grabbed her torch. "Come on then. If we're going, let's get it done." She walked over to the table by the window, picked up the phone that was there and carried it back to the sofa. The cord only just stretched far enough. "Call the police," she told Mick, "and tell them what's going on, if they'll believe you. Even if they don't, hopefully they'll send someone out here to check. And call an ambulance too, while you're at it. I don't want you dying on us just because I can't wrap a bandage right."

Mick nodded. "Be careful you two."

"We will be," Dan assured him. He looked at Jenny and she nodded. Together they went outside. Jenny looked at the road stretching ahead of them.

Time to expose your secrets, Haven. They've been hidden for far too long.

CHAPTER SEVENTEEN

As they hurried along the main road, Jenny glanced up the side road that led to Ash Lodge and stopped.

What if I don't get another chance to see my mother? What if I die out here and I never get to say goodbye? The urge to run to the lodge, throw open the door and hug her mother tightly was almost overwhelming, but Jenny forced herself to start walking again. If she burst into the house, Pamela would want to know why; and if she knew why, she'd never let Jenny out of the house again. Jenny didn't want the deaths of Thomas and Samuel on her hands.

"You okay?" Dan asked.

"I'm fine. Let's just keeping going."

As they headed towards Samuel's lodge, Jenny constantly looked around. Too many shadows appeared to be moving. She felt that familiar pressure on her chest again and her breathing began to speed up. She forced herself to keep calm. The cold nipped at every spot of exposed skin.

They turned up the side road leading to Samuel's lodge. The porch light flickered on as they approached and Jenny stopped dead. Dan did too. They stared at the door. There were deep grooves in it. Something had tried to claw its way inside.

Jenny saw her own trepidation mirrored in Dan's face. "Should we go in?" he asked.

She knelt down, running her fingers along the grooves. Splinters of jagged wood threatened to catch in her skin. *Bloody hell, her nails must have been sharp to do that. And she must be very strong.*

She stood up and said decidedly, "Yes, let's go in. It doesn't look like the creature got in. Maybe Samuel's in there, maybe he isn't, but we need to check."

They tried to door, but it was locked. They did a circuit of the lodge, trying the back door and all the windows, but there was no way in. They peered into the dark interior but, if Samuel was in there, they couldn't see him.

"Come on," said Jenny eventually, "let's try Thomas."

Dan's face was pale in the moonlight. He hesitated, for just a fraction of a second, then nodded.

Back on the main road, the lights were playing up. When Jenny and Dan passed the motion sensors, the lights above them came on weak and flickering.

Dan rubbed his chest. "You feel that?"

Jenny nodded. It felt like there was a belt around her breastbone that was slowly being tightened. "It's Marguerite's spells. Which means her daughter must be close."

They reached Thomas's lodge and Dan banged on the door. Anna opened it, looking surprised.

"We need to speak to Thomas," Dan said urgently.

Anna's eyes came to rest suspiciously on Jenny. "Why? What's he done?"

The door was pulled open further and Thomas stepped past his wife.

"We know. About Marguerite," Dan said bluntly. "We know you had an affair with her."

The colour drained from Thomas's face. He turned slightly, as if to look round at his wife, and then thought better of it. "I don't—"

"We know you got her pregnant," Jenny added.

Thomas's mouth snapped shut. Now he did glance

over his shoulder at Anna, whose look was one of pure hatred. He stepped out and closed the door behind him. Colour returned to his face, his cheeks red with rage. He sneered at them. "You're a nasty pair of troublemakers, you two. A nasty pair. Now, I want you get off my porch and—"

"Pair," Dan said. His eyes were unfocussed. He creased his brow. "Pair. That's what the boy said, before you killed him." His gaze sharpened and he stared at Thomas. His voice became hard and full of hatred. "Only it wasn't "pair", was it? He said "peré", he called you father, in the only language he knew how. You knew, didn't you, Thomas, when he said that? You knew he was Marguerite's child, *your* child. You knew and you murdered him all the same."

Thomas's mouth opened and closed, but no sound came out. Then he seemed to gather himself and said coldly, "That creature was no son of mine. It was a filthy, deformed—"

Dan punched him. Thomas reeled back, gripping his cheek. His face showed first shock then fury. He stepped towards Dan. "Why you little—"

"Enough!" Jenny stepped between them, a hand on each of their chests. Their heartbeats were both fast against her fingertips. "There are other, more important things to talk about."

But Dan wasn't done yet. "Wasn't it your own wife who told everyone that the offspring of extra-marital affairs were creatures of sin? I guess there's living proof of that out in the woods."

"That thing's deformity has nothing to do with me. Marguerite was a witch. It's her fault he's a monster."

"We haven't got time for this," Jenny repeated

109

forcefully. "We came to warn you, Thomas. There's another creature out there. Marguerite gave birth to a boy *and* a girl. We killed the boy and now the girl is coming after us. She hunts by smell. She got Mick. He's badly wounded but safe in his house. He's called an ambulance and the police, but we need to make sure everyone stays safe until they get here."

Thomas drew himself up. "It wouldn't dare come after me. I'm—"

"You're what?" Jenny snapped, her patience gone. "You think this thing cares about your status here? She lives by instinct and hunts by smell. Her instinct brought her to her brother's corpse, and our stink on it will lead her to each of us. Now, if you want to be useful, you can tell us where Samuel is. We tried his house but it was locked and empty."

Thomas looked at her through narrowed eyes. "If you're looking for Samuel, you might want to try Ash Lodge. In the bushes." He gave a lecherous grin.

It all came together in her mind: the flattened undergrowth around the lodge; Thomas bumping into Samuel and whispering to him, "Your flies are undone."

Fury boiled up in Jenny. She launched herself at him, but Dan caught her and held her back.

"You piece of shit! He's been spying on me and my mum, and you bloody well knew about it?"

Thomas held his hands up. "I told him not to, but he kept insisting. I figured Mick would catch him soon enough and then it would be over." He dropped his hands, a sneer curling his lips. "Besides, he's only looking, what's the harm?"

Jenny struggled in Dan's grip, but his arms tightened around her. "Come on," he urged, "we've got more important things to do."

Thomas gave her a triumphant grin, before going back inside. Dan released Jenny and she turned on him angrily. "You think I want to save that pervert when he's been spying on me and my mother?"

"Jenny, you're angry. Yeah, Samuel's a piece of shit, Thomas too, but neither of them deserve to be ripped apart. You've seen this creature, and so have I. Death at her hands would... well, it wouldn't be a very good way to go." A haunted look came into his eyes, and that more than anything dampened her anger. Jenny took a moment to calm herself, then reluctantly followed him.

As they walked along the main road, the lights were even weaker than before; that fact gave added speed to their steps. Jenny's heart was fluttering as they approached Ash Lodge. Dan called out Samuel's name, telling him that he was in danger and that they needed to talk to him. Jenny merely walked mutely by his side, still unsure whether Samuel was worth saving if he'd been out here spying on them.

They were halfway through a circuit of the lodge when they found him, the source of a large pool of blood seeping among the trees. Samuel's throat had been ripped out; there were bite-marks on his face. His eyes were open, staring at nothing. His hand was still inside his trousers.

Jenny turned away, fighting down the urge to vomit. When she'd gathered herself she said, "Come on. I don't want to stay here and put Mum in danger. There's nothing we can do for him now anyway. The police can deal with him when they get here. Let's get ourselves to safety, that's the most important thing."

CHAPTER EIGHTEEN

As Dan knocked on Thomas's door for the second time that night, the image of Samuel with his throat a raw, bloody mess was still forefront in his mind.

Shit! How can things have gotten this bad? Mick's injured. Samuel's dead. She'll be coming for us next. We need to get to safety, fast.

The door opened and Thomas stood there, red-faced and breathing heavily. From behind him came the crash of crockery against a wall. Thomas pulled the door close to his body, blocking their view past him.

"Did you find Samuel?"

"Yes. He's dead. She got him," Dan replied.

Thomas's shoulders slumped; he looked a decade older. "Oh god. Poor Samuel."

"We need to stick together," Jenny said flatly. "Safety in numbers. This creature is smart. She lured Mick into the woods and then she got Samuel when he was alone as well. We've more chance of fighting her off until the police get here if we stay together."

"And what then?" Thomas snapped. "When the police arrive it'll just disappear into the forest, bide its time, then come for us again when we least expect it."

"So what do you suggest?" Dan asked.

"We have to find a way to kill it. Tonight," Thomas said firmly.

Dan stared at him incredulously. "Seriously? That's your daughter, Thomas. And the only reason we're in this bloody mess is because you killed her brother."

Thomas didn't appear to hear him; his eyes were feverishly bright. "We should lure it into a trap."

Jenny folded her arms, disdain clear on her face. "Lure it with what precisely?"

At that moment, the door was wrenched from Thomas's grip. Thomas backed onto the porch, away from Anna, who stood in the doorway. Her hair was a mess and she wore a cruel smile. "You need bait to lure it? Well, how about this bastard right here?" She shoved Thomas so hard that he stumbled backwards down the porch steps and landed heavily on the ground.

She sneered at him. "I told you that the offspring of your affairs would be monstrous, and I was right. And now you must pay for your sins at the hands of your own progeny. Go find your witch's children before they find you!"

Anna slammed the door. Dan heard the key click in the lock. Thomas ran up the steps and banged on the door, screaming at his wife.

Dan turned to Jenny. "Where to?"

"The main hall," she said firmly. "The kitchen's there. We can get knives and other stuff to defend ourselves."

They grabbed Thomas and hauled him off the steps. He was shouting blue murder, but followed them nonetheless.

"That bitch! Did you see what she did? By God, when this is over I'll—"

"We're going to the main hall, Thomas," Jenny said firmly. "Either come with us or take your chances on your own."

Thomas's gaze flicked between them. He straightened up then strode past them. Dan exchanged a look with Jenny, then they followed. They reached the main road, but as they walked down it, none of the lights came on.

"What the hell is this?" hissed Thomas.

"Feel that? Against your chest?" Jenny asked.

Thomas rubbed his chest and winced. "What is it?"

"Your daughter is out to get us," Jenny said darkly, "and her mother's spells are going to help her do it."

CHAPTER NINETEEN

Thomas glared at them. "What the hell are you talking about? Marguerite's dead."

Jenny stopped dead and glared at him. "And how would you know that, Thomas? I thought you and Samuel escorted her off the land.

Thomas's face went slack. "I... well, I—"

"You're a piece of shit, Thomas," Dan snarled. He turned to Jenny. "I say we leave him here."

Thomas grabbed Jenny's arm, his face twisted in fear. "No, please don't."

Jenny yanked her arm away. "Come with us or don't. Right now, I really don't care either way."

Jenny walked ahead, Dan by her side. A moment later, Thomas was on the other side.

"What was all that about Marguerite?" Thomas asked.

"Later," Jenny said. "Let's just get to safety first, then we'll tell you all about the mess you got us in."

Thomas scowled, but didn't push it. As they passed another dead light, he asked in a quieter voice, "Should we turn our torches on?"

"No. It's a clear night. There's a moon. We can see fine. If we turn our torches on, that will draw her right to us, if she doesn't know where we are already. And I don't think torches will help us much if she attacks."

"Except as a weapon," Dan pointed out.

They continued along the road, trying to balance walking fast with walking quietly. Jenny tensed every time a stone crunched under her shoe. As they drew closer to the door of the main hut, all three of them sped up. Dan reached the door first. He tried the handle but it was locked. "What do we do now?" he whispered.

"The back door," Thomas said decisively. "It'll be locked as well but there's a key underneath a stone by—"

His words were cut off as a black shape cannoned into him, knocking him backwards. Jenny was already raising her torch to strike but before she had a chance, Thomas's attacker fled into the darkness.

Thomas grasped at his side. Blood oozed through his fingers. "The little bitch!"

"Come on. Round the back," Jenny urged. They raced round the hall to the back door.

Dan seized the door handle and twisted, but the door was locked. He turned to Thomas. "Where's the key?"

Awkwardly and wincing with pain, Thomas knelt down by the flowerbed that ran the length of the wall and lifted up a plastic rock. He turned it over and slid back a hatch, revealing the key. He gave the key to Jenny who hurried to the door. Her hands were shaking so much that it took her several attempts to fit the key in the lock.

There was a scream behind her and the terrible crack of bones. Jenny turned in time to see a dark shape disappearing into the night as Dan sank to his knees, his face white and his shoulder dislocated and hunched up to his ear. "My shoulder, God, my shoulder," he moaned. He touched it with his other hand and screamed in agony.

"Don't worry," Jenny said, her voice hoarse, "I've almost got the door open."

The creature darted out of the shadows again, this time towards Thomas. But instead of dodging it, Thomas opened his arms and grabbed the feral girl as she jumped at him.

"Got you, you little bitch. Argh!" The creature had bitten down hard on his arm. Thomas grabbed her hair and yanked back. Her head came away, but so did a big chunk of his flesh.

The girl hissed and sprang away, leaving Thomas holding a handful of hair. It looked like she was fleeing, but then she circled round and ran straight at Thomas again.

The two of them became a tumbling mass of arms and legs as they fell to the floor and rolled. When they came to a stop, the feral girl pinned Thomas to the ground. She lifted her head then brought it down as fast as a striking snake. Thomas jerked away at the last second so that the creature sank her jaws into his cheek. Blood, black beneath the moonlight, spread over his face. Thomas grappled with the girl, trying to push her off. Her head snapped down a second time and her teeth sank into the place where his shoulder met his neck. Thomas screamed, loud and shrill.

Jenny rushed towards them. She raised her torch and brought it down on the girl's back. The girl squeaked and let go of Thomas to turn on Jenny with a snarl. Jenny brought the torch down again, aiming for the girl's head. The girl twisted so Jenny landed a blow on her shoulder. The impact sent a painful judder up Jenny's arm.

The girl staggered off Thomas who rolled away, moaning. She crouched, her eyes fixed on Jenny, ready to leap. Not giving her time, Jenny stepped forward and brought the torch down again. The girl hesitated, uncertain whether to spring or defend herself, and that hesitation robbed her of the chance to do either. The blow caught her on the cheek, sending her spinning sideways.

Jenny didn't think, she just kept moving, bringing the torch down again and again as the girl tried to crawl away.

Jenny's heart was pounding, her breathing was ragged; she was fuelled by fear.

The girl twisted onto her back and looked up. Her dark eyes were wide. Her mouth was smeared with Thomas's blood, while her own blood seeped over her cheek from a wound Jenny had inflicted.

The girl extended a hand as Jenny raised the torch to deliver a final blow. Jenny hesitated. In her mind, she saw the boy raising his arm to Thomas in just the same way.

"Jenny. Don't." Dan's voice was no more than a whisper, but it cut through the haze in Jenny's mind. She pushed aside her fear and anger to look properly at the world around her. The girl lying on the ground was breathing shallowly. Her eyes were wide with fear, while her lips curled in a snarl. Her whole body was shaking.

She killed Samuel. She was going to kill all of us.

But then, we killed her brother, her only companion.

She's just a girl.

Jenny lowered the torch, eyeing the girl warily. She didn't put it past the creature to leap at her now that her defences were down. The girl slowly drew her arm back, watching Jenny with equal caution. Beyond the matted hair Jenny saw a girl about her own age, filthy and feral, but still just a girl, driven by anger.

Not so different from me when you get down to it.

Jenny took a deep, steadying breath. "I don't know if you can understand me, but the police will be here soon and they'll be able to take you somewhere safe and you—"

Thomas pushed her roughly aside. One hand clamped over his neck wound, his fingers shining with blood; the other hand held a rock which he raised up high. Before Jenny could stop him, he brought the rock crashing down on the girl's head. The girl's eyes widened with pain and she spasmed, her whole body drawing in on itself like a dead spider. Then her arms flopped onto the grass, her head rolled to the side and she was still.

Jenny stared at Thomas as he sank to the ground, the rock tumbling from his fingers. His face was unnaturally white. His clothes were soaked with blood. His hand fell limply away from his neck and blood poured out of the wound.

"You killed... your daughter." Jenny had to force the words out, her throat tight. The pressure across her chest was immense.

Thomas looked up at her, his eyes dazed with pain. He was panting. Blood trickled out of his mouth as he spoke. "It was... monstrous. I... had to..."

He swayed, closed his eyes then toppled to the ground. Blood spilled from his wound ever more slowly to form a pool on the grass.

"She's not the one who's monstrous," Jenny said, the words coming through breathlessly. The pressure on her chest was unbearable. She dropped the torch, her arms as heavy as lead. She clawed at her throat. Blackness was creeping across the edges of her vision — and then the sensation vanished.

Jenny gulped in air, her lungs burning at the sudden cold of it. Her breath huffed in a roiling mist. She started to shiver as an unnatural chill spread through her. Her skin prickled and, with absolute certainty, she knew someone was standing at her shoulder.

"Dan?" she asked, trying to keep her teeth from chattering. She felt a shift in the air, as if someone was leaning closer to her.

"Marguerite," she whispered. Trembling, Jenny stared

straight ahead. "I'm sorry about your daughter, Marguerite, and your son.

"I understand now. That stuff left on my porch — that was an offering, wasn't it? Your son was trying to reach out to me. And in the woods that night, when he took my hand, he wasn't going to kill me, was he? I bet he saw us and had all these feelings and had no idea what to do, didn't he?"

There was a hiss and cold hair ruffled Jenny's hair.

"They shouldn't have beat him for it and Thomas shouldn't have killed him, or her. I wish I could change that, but I can't."

Another breath curled around her, stronger this time. It carried the stink of the grave, so much worse than the ammonia-laden stench of the feral children.

"There's nothing left for you, Marguerite. Your children are dead and so are you". I'm sorry for my part in it, but it's done. Now, please go away and leave us alone."

Jenny's ears were ringing in the silence. The presence hadn't left her shoulder. Jenny clenched her fists, pushing aside her fear to dredge up as much anger as she could. "Fuck off, Marguerite. You have no place here."

A gust of icy wind rushed around her and then was gone. Fighting to control the trembling that was in every limb, Jenny slowly turned round. No one stood behind her. Dan was slumped against the wall of the main hut, his face pale.

With difficulty, he walked towards her. "What was that?"

"Marguerite, I think. Did you see her?"

"Something that looked like her but also like it was just shadows and I was seeing something that wasn't there." He frowned. "My head's spinning and I can't explain it any better that."

Jenny wasn't sure that she wanted to know any more detail anyway. She turned back to the two bodies lying on the grass, to find that there was only one. The girl's body had gone.

Jenny frantically spun around, searching the darkness for any sign of the girl. "Where is she? Did she crawl off? Did Marguerite take her?"

"I don't know. I didn't see."

"But she can't be alive. You don't survive head blows like that, do you?" She looked at Dan. He opened his mouth then shut it again. They stood for a moment, just looking at each other, trying to comprehend what had just happened.

Feeling numb inside and out, Jenny and Dan made their way round the side of the building. The main road that they'd run down in darkness was now lit up by the flashing lights of police cars and an ambulance.

"No more secrets now, Haven," she muttered. And yet, the darkness still seemed to press close around her.

CHAPTER TWENTY

Jenny reached for the last of the bags, but another hand beat hers to it. She looked up at Dan, who winced as he hoisted the bag into the boot of Pamela's car.

"Are you sure you should be lifting things?" Jenny asked.

Rather than answer the question, Dan said, "I couldn't let you go without saying goodbye."

"I thought we did that in there?" she asked, nodding towards the main hut. People were gradually coming out, congregating to wave them off.

"Yeah, but I figured you deserved better than that, what with saving my life and all last week."

Jenny looked away, uncomfortable. "I don't think I saved anyone's life. Samuel died, Thomas died, the girl died, and her brother."

"But you didn't kill her, or her brother."

"No, but then I didn't manage to stop Thomas doing it either." She bit her lip. "Do you think she's dead?"

Dan glanced down, scuffing the tarmac with his shoe. "I don't know. I know she didn't deserve to die and all, but the thought that she might still be out there, watching us, makes me feel scared in ways I never thought possible."

"You need to get out of here, Dan."

He looked up and smiled. "No, I don't. Haven is my home. It's not been a very good one so far, but with Samuel and Thomas gone, I'm going to make it better. Well, I'm going to try anyway." His face grew serious. "I'll miss you though."

A wave of emotion washed over Jenny and she threw her arms around him, hugging him tightly. "Come visit anytime, you'll always be welcome."

They broke apart and he wiped tears off his lashes. "Definitely."

Pamela's approach ended their conversation. Jenny gave Dan another, more gentle hug. Then she climbed into the car and buckled up. Her mother turned to her. "Ready?"

"Ready," Jenny said confidently. "And Mum — next time *I* get to pick where we move to."

Pamela grinned. "Absolutely no argument from me there."

As the car drove round the fountain, both Jenny and Pamela waved at the gathered crowd.

We're off to a new life. Or maybe we'll pick up the old one where we left off. Jenny realised she didn't care, so long as she was far away from Haven.

Dan made his way back into the main hut with the others, his heart heavy.

He was barely through the door when someone stepped in front of him. It was Anna. She'd remained inside, refusing to wave goodbye to Pamela and Jenny. She was a shadow of her old self, her clothes crumpled and her hair greasy, but her eyes still burned with malice.

"I saw you hug that slut. I'm surprised. I didn't think your kind were into female contact. Or is she a — what do they call them? Hag?"

Fury heated Dan's blood. He pressed his lips tightly together, trying to keep back the insults threatening to pour forth.

No, that's not me. I don't keep silent. Not anymore.

He stepped forward. Anna's eyes widened. He smiled. "You're quite right, Anna. "My kind" aren't really into female contact. And yes, girls who are friends with gay men are called "hags", or rather "fag hags" to be precise. But if you ask me, I'd say that Jenny isn't really the hag around here."

Anna's mouth dropped open. She took three steps back, staring at him as if he carried something contagious. Dan realised that everyone in the room was watching him. It made his skin itch, but he stood his ground.

A hand squeezed his shoulder. It was his mother. "I'd have to agree with my son on that point."

Anna sneered. "Agree with him? You should be ashamed of him, Selena, not standing up for him."

"Well, I don't really care what you think," Selena said, "he's my son and I love him."

"Have you lost your mind?" Anna snapped, spittle spraying from her mouth. "He's an abomination. He should get out. Out!"

Dan tensed, his stomach cramping painfully. The world seemed to be going fuzzy around the edges.

At the back of the hall, Millicent stood up from her seat. "Yes, I agree," she said loudly. Dan felt as if the world was spiralling away from him. "The lad should get out. It's not good for him to be here, with no one his own age. There's a course on agriculture at Alnwick college, only part-time but I think he should sign up for it, make some friends, learn a bit, then come back and use what he knows here in Haven. We'd all be better for it."

"That's not what I meant, you stupid old woman," Anna snarled.

Esme came to stand by her sister, the two of them staring at Anna. "We know what you meant," Esme said quietly.

Anna's jaw dropped. "But *he's* even more of monster than the thing they killed."

"Is he, though, Anna?" Millicent said mildly, cocking her head slightly. "Is he the one that's a monster here?"

Murmurs ran around the hall, heads nodded. Dan stared at them, his whole body trembling. Selena stepped closer, putting an arm around him.

Anna gave a wild, throaty laugh. "You're all so wrapped up in sin, you can't see it, can you?"

She spun on her heel and stormed out.

Dan was aware of every eye in the room on him. He turned to look at his mother who was smiling, tears in her eyes.

"I've got to go," he muttered, a sob choking up his throat. He hurried out of the hut and into the sunlight outside. He took in deep gulps of fresh air.

Mick came up behind him. "Let's take a walk to my place."

His mind frozen, his limbs shaking, Dan followed without question. As he walked by the old man's side, the world gradually came back into focus.

They walked in silence until they reached Mick's gate. "Two monsters dealt with in one week," Mick said, as he leaned back against his gate, taking in the forest.

"Do you think I did the right thing?" Dan asked, slumping back against the gate. "Maybe I shouldn't have said anything."

Mick snorted. "It's not like we have a choice in these matters, despite what some would have us believe. You told everyone a fact, simple as that. Either they'll accept it or they won't. And from what I heard, nobody had a problem with it or you. Well, apart from one of them, but she doesn't count, not any more. Mind you, if you're looking for bile, you should have heard what my mother said when I came out. That's why I don't swear any more, I had my fill of it that day."

Dan looked sidelong at him. "You said fuck Anna and fuck Thomas."

Mick shifted uncomfortably. "Well, those two bring it out in a man."

They both fell silent, looking at the forest. The bluebells were on the way out, but they still provided a vibrant blue carpet beneath a spreading, verdant canopy. Dan wondered if the feral girl was still alive and out there now, watching them and waiting for her chance to strike again. Or whether, like him and so many others, she was just trying to find a quiet spot to survive in a world that didn't understand her at all.

Acknowledgements & Bio

As with all books, this one would never have seen the light of day without the help of many people. First up is my editor, Peter: thanks for taking a chance and bearing with me while I ironed out the kinks. Thanks to David for reading through the eventual first draft and pointing out the bits where I made my characters sound like they were punctured ketchup bottles. Thanks also to Jim, who also read the first draft and made me feel I might actually have written something decent. And thank you to N&S for not minding when I buried my head in a book for research, or disappeared somewhere quiet to dream up nightmares.

.

Charlotte Bond
Leeds
April 2017

Bio: Charlotte has been published within the genres of horror, fantasy, science fiction. She is also a ghostwriter, but she's not allowed to tell you about those books. Charlotte is a reviewer for the Ginger Nuts of Horror website and also a co-host of the podcast, Breaking the Glass Slipper. She lives in West Yorkshire, as it's not practical to live in North Yorkshire. Online, she lives at www.charlottebond.co.uk

Hersham Horror Books

http://silenthater.wix.com/hersham-horror-books#

70724780R00079

Made in the USA
Columbia, SC
12 May 2017